American Heritag[e]
Migration & Immigration History Activities

Author: Schyrlet Cameron
Editor: Mary Dieterich
Contributor: Karl Mechem
Proofreaders: Alexis Fey and Margaret Brown

COPYRIGHT © 2022 Mark Twain Media, Inc.

ISBN 978-1-62223-879-8

Printing No. CD-405078

Mark Twain Media, Inc., Publishers
Distributed by Carson Dellosa Education

The purchase of this book entitles the buyer to reproduce the student pages for classroom use only. Other permissions may be obtained by writing Mark Twain Media, Inc., Publishers.

All rights reserved. Printed in the United States of America.

Visit us at www.marktwainpublishing.com

Table of Contents

Introduction to the Teacher 1

Unit One: Major Migration Events
   What Is Migration? 2
   Prehistoric Migration to the Americas..4
   The Industrial Revolution 6
   Settlement Beyond the Appalachian Mountains 8
   Manifest Destiny...10
   Oregon Fever...12
   The California Gold Rush 14
   Homestead Act of 1862...16
   Oklahoma Land Rush 18
   The Great Migration 20
   The Dust Bowl...22
   Recent Shifts in Population 24

Unit Two: Major Immigration Events
   What Is Immigration?...26
   The Four Waves of Immigration..28
   Colonial Era..30
   Importation of Enslaved Africans...32
   The Irish Potato Famine..34
   The Transcontinental Railroad 36
   The Chinese Exclusion Act 38
   World War I 40
   World War II..42

Unit Three: Coming to America
   Immigration Laws..44
   The Statue of Liberty...46
   Immigration Stations 48
   National Immigrant Heritage Month 50

Unit Four: United States Citizenship
   The Constitution and Citizenship 52
   Naturalization 54
   Rights and Responsibilities of Citizenship 56

Answer Keys..58

Introduction to the Teacher

The United States is often characterized as a "nation of immigrants." It is important for the future of America to produce good citizens. In order to be good citizens, we must first gain a basic knowledge of our history and the role of immigration in forming our nation.

Migration & Immigration History Activities is one of several books in Mark Twain Media's *American Heritage Series* for grades 5 through 8. The content and activities are designed to strengthen student understanding of the major migration and immigration events of the United States.

The study of history is important because if we don't know where we have been, we have no way to understand the present or predict the future. We should not try to hide from the past, even the unpleasant parts, so the bad decisions that were made have been included along with those that brought achievement and growth. Progress for our nation depends on how we as individuals and groups evaluate our decisions and react to the decisions of others. Wise decisions pull us up; foolish decisions push us down. As humans, we are all capable of both.

How the Book Is Organized

The book text is presented in an easy-to-read format that does not overwhelm the struggling reader. Vocabulary words are boldfaced. The lessons provide challenging activities that promote reading, critical thinking, and writing skills.

The 28 lessons contained in *Migration & Immigration History Activities* cover four units of study: *Major Migration Events, Major Immigration Events, Coming to America,* and *United States Citizenship.* The units can be used in the order presented or in an order that best fits the classroom or home school curriculum. Teachers can easily differentiate units to address individual learning levels and needs. Each lesson consists of two pages.
- **Reading Selection:** identifies the basic waves of migration and immigration and push and pull factors of major events.
- **Activity Page:** checks the reader's comprehension.

Push and Pull Factors

Throughout the book, the terms *push factors* and *pull factors* are used. These refer to the reasons why people relocate from one area to a home in another area. **Push factors** are conditions that "push" people away from their homes and include such things as too few jobs, wars, and natural disasters. **Pull factors** are conditions that "pull" people to a new home and include things such as safety, jobs, higher wages, and the promise of a better life.

National and State Standards

Migration & Immigration History Activities promotes the current national and state standards. It is written for classroom teachers, parents, and students. It is designed as stand-alone material for classrooms and homeschooling. Also, the book can be used as a supplemental resource to enhance the history curriculum for the classroom, independent study, or home tutorial.

Front Cover Identification:

(Center image) Statue of Liberty; (Clockwise from top right) Ellis Island Immigration Station; Immigrants sailing past the Statue of Liberty; Naturalization ceremony; the Arthur family arriving in Chicago; Immgrants arriving in the United States; Angel Island Immigration Station; Westward migration

What Is Migration?

People have always been on the move in the United States. During the Industrial Revolution in the 1700s, large numbers of people moved from country areas to towns and cities. During the 1800s, settlers moved to new land in the West. After the Civil War, thousands of African Americans moved from the South to the North. Today, many people living in the northern states migrate to the southern states during the winter months.

Migration in the United States

The mass movement of a population within a country or region is referred to as **migration**. Migration can be voluntary or forced. It can take place over short or long distances, and it can be a permanent or temporary move.

Kinds of Migration
- **Animal Migration:** Some animals stay in the same place their entire lives, others migrate just once in their lives, and still others migrate every year. For example, Snow Geese migrate south in winter and north in summer. Each year Snow geese fly south to avoid the winter freeze of lakes and ponds. Then they return for the summer to breed and nest.
- **Human Migration:** Great numbers of people moving from one region of the United States to another have taken place throughout the history of our nation. For example, the Great Migration was the movement of over six million African Americans from the southern states of the United States to the northern states in the 1900s.

Push and Pull Factors

There are any number of reasons why people relocate from one area to a home in another area. These are referred to as push and pull factors. **Push factors** are conditions that "push" people away from their homes and include such things as too few jobs, wars, and natural disasters. **Pull factors** are conditions that "pull" people to a new home and include things such as safety, jobs, higher wages, and the promise of a better life.

Migration vs. Immigration

People move between various regions, switching cities, countries, or even parts of the world. Both immigration and migration refer to this movement of people. You might wonder how to distinguish between immigration and migration.
- **Migration** refers to the movement of a large population of people from one area to another within a country or region. For example, the Homestead Act of 1862 encouraged western migration in the United States by providing settlers with 160 acres of land for a small filing fee. Thousands of people moved to the Great Plains to take advantage of the free land.
- **Immigration** refers to the process of moving to another country to live permanently. For example, Americans encouraged relatively free and open immigration during the 18th and early 19th centuries. From 1845 to 1849, Ireland's potato crop failed, causing a famine. Thousands of Irish people came to the United States to escape starvation.

Name: _____ Date: _____

Activity: Word Meaning

Directions: Use information from the reading selection to complete the page. Write a definition for each word and use each word in a sentence.

| **Migration** | Definition: |
| | Sentence: |

| **Immigration** | Definition: |
| | Sentence: |

| **Push Factors** | Definition: |
| | Sentence: |

| **Pull Factors** | Definition: |
| | Sentence: |

Prehistoric Migration to the Americas

Although the names of those who first moved to North America are not recorded, we do know a little about them and how they traveled. The first people to arrive in the Americas didn't sail here in large ships—they walked thousands of miles across Siberia in Asia to present-day Alaska in North America.

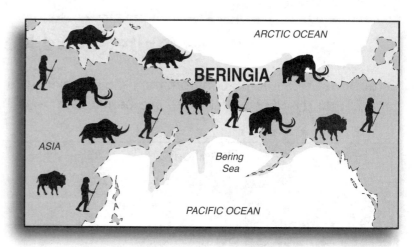

Scientists believe the Bering land bridge from Asia to North America was a route of animal and human migration beginning about 30,000 years ago.

Last Ice Age

The earth has passed through several **Ice Ages**, times of freezing temperatures. During the last Ice Age, two-mile-thick sheets of ice called **ice caps** formed. These giant ice caps covered both the Arctic and Antarctic regions of the earth. The levels of the oceans lowered because much of the earth's water was trapped in the polar ice caps. The lower water level exposed a piece of land between Asia and North America. This land bridge was a thousand miles wide. Today this area is once again underwater and is called the Bering Strait. The Bering land bridge disappeared under the water when the ice caps thawed around 8,000 B.C.

Crossing the Bering Land Bridge

Scientists believe the land bridge was free of ice and covered in grass. Herds of hairy elephants called mammoths and giant bison from Asia came to graze. Stone Age people followed the grass-eating animals across the land bridge. This mass movement of people and animals from one region to another is called **migration**.

These early people depended on the animals for their food, clothing, and shelter. They knew how to use fire. Without it, they might not have survived. With it, they could stay warm and cook meat. These early people were the ancestors of the what are today called Native Americans or First Nations peoples.

Migration

Small groups began arriving in North America about 30,000 years ago. As they traveled, groups might settle for a time in a place that offered good hunting or fishing. Some stayed for a year or two or even many years before moving on. Eventually, some of the group or their descendants continued the journey, following the migrating herds of animals they hunted into the eastern parts of North America. In time, some of these hunting people went as far south as the tip of South America.

Not all groups made the journey at the same time. Many waves of migrants crossed the land bridge during a period covering more than 25,000 years. By the time Christopher Columbus set sail from Spain in 1492, thousands of groups of people with many different cultures and languages lived in the Americas.

Migration & Immigration History Activities | Unit One: Prehistoric Migration to the Americas

Name: _____ Date: _____

Activity: Summarizing

Directions: Use information from the reading selection to complete the graphic organizer.

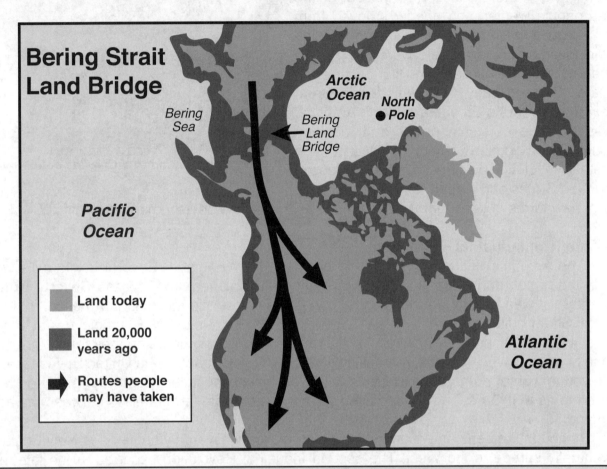

Prehistoric Migration to the Americas	
Key Details	**Summary**

The Industrial Revolution

The **Industrial Revolution** was the time in history when the production of **goods**, or the things people wanted and needed, moved from small shops and homes to large factories using power-driven machinery. There were two phases to the Industrial Revolution. The first occurred in the late 17th and early 18th centuries in Great Britain and spread to Europe and North America. It was the age of steam power and machine production of goods. The second phase of the Industrial Revolution occurred in the mid-1800s in the United States and spread to Europe. It was a time of new forms of transportation, communication, and the development of electricity.

A young girl working in a Carolina cotton mill in 1908

The American Industrial Revolution

The American Industrial Revolution began in New England. Several textile mills were built in the region during the late 18th and early 19th centuries. In 1787, the **Beverly Cotton Manufactory** was built in Massachusetts. It was the first textile mill built in America. In 1793, **Samuel Slater** built a textile mill in Pawtucket, Rhode Island. Almost all 30 employees at the mill were children. In those days, children were already working long hours on their family farms, so no one objected to their working in a mill. In 1823, the first factories in the United States to begin hiring young women were the textile mills in Lowell, Massachusetts. These young women were referred to as **Mill Girls**. The mill recruited young women from farm families between the ages of 15 and 35.

Although the early American Industrial Revolution was largely confined to New England, it eventually spread to the West. The second Industrial Revolution occurred in the late 19th century and spread to the South.

Migration From Farm to City

Migration is the mass movement of people from one region to another. Approximately 11 million people moved from rural to urban areas during the Industrial Revolution in America. The migration of people from rural to urban areas is called **urbanization**. Today, most Americans live in **urban** areas, or areas around cities. However, from colonial times to the late 1700s, most people lived in **rural** areas, or the countryside. During the Industrial Revolution, people migrated to the cities to work in factories.

Results of the Industrial Revolution

Industrialization, or the process of using power-driven machinery for manufacturing goods, provided tremendous benefits for people. Inventions and advancements in technology improved people's lives. It also created great hardships. The growth of factories created a demand for labor, but workers were made to work long hours and often in unsafe conditions. Many people left the farm and moved to the cities for paying jobs. Cities grew and became overcrowded.

Migration & Immigration History Activities — Unit One: The Industrial Revolution

Name: _____ Date: _____

Activity: Word Meaning

Directions: Use information from the reading selection to complete the graphic organizer.

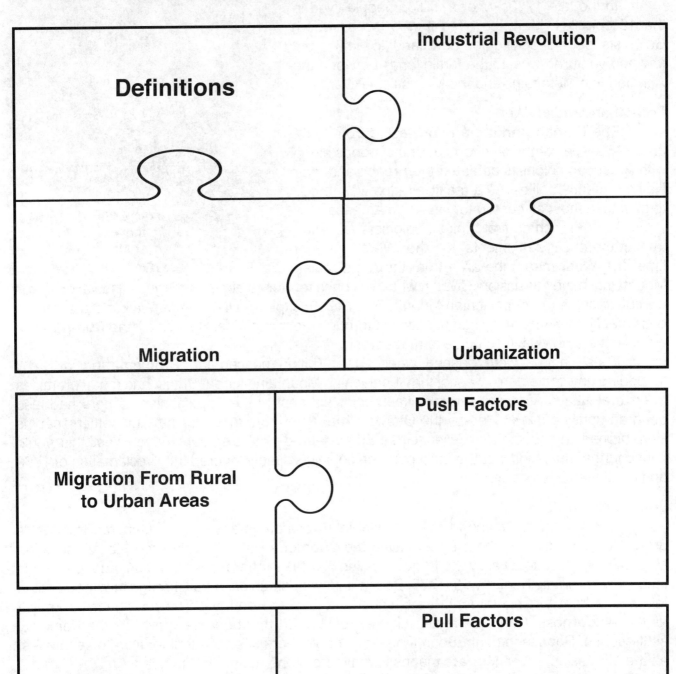

Definitions

Industrial Revolution

Migration

Urbanization

Push Factors

Migration From Rural to Urban Areas

Pull Factors

Migration From Rural to Urban Areas

Settlement Beyond the Appalachian Mountains

In the late 1700s, over 2 million people lived in the 13 colonies. Many believed it was too crowded. Colonists began looking for new land to settle, but few had ventured west to the fertile lands between the Appalachian Mountains and the Mississippi River.

1754 British Colonies and Appalachian Mountains

French and Indian War

The **French and Indian War** lasted from 1754 until 1763. The combined efforts of British troops along with American colonists defeated the French and their Native American allies. As a result, France was forced to give up almost all her territory in North America.

With French control broken, colonists expected to expand their settlements to "the West." At that time, **the West** meant the area from the Appalachian Mountains to the Mississippi River in what was once territory claimed by France. However, it was difficult to cross the Appalachian Mountains. In 1750, explorer Dr. Thomas Walker discovered a pass that Native Americans had used to cut through the mountains. He called it the **Cumberland Gap**. Settlers now saw a chance to move west.

Those hopes were dashed when Great Britain passed the **Proclamation of 1763** forbidding any settlements west of the Appalachian Mountains. Great Britain had made promises to several Native American tribes to keep colonists east of the Appalachians. There had also been an uprising in 1763 led by the Ottawa **Chief Pontiac** during which many settlers' cabins were burned and people were killed. Great Britain feared if more settlers moved west, this would cause further uprisings. For the most part, the colonists simply ignored the Proclamation of 1763 and continued to move west.

Wilderness Trail

During the French and Indian War, Daniel Boone drove a wagon for General Braddock's army. He heard stories about a trail called the "Warrior's Path" that crossed the Appalachian Mountains and led to a valley the Iroquois called **Kentake**. After the war, Boone tried to find this land, now known as Kentucky. In 1775, Boone and woodsmen cut a trail through the Appalachian Mountains from Virginia through the Cumberland Gap to Kentucky. The path became known as the **Wilderness Trail**. Boone and his men built a fort that became known as the Kentucky settlement of Boonesborough. Soon thousands of pioneers used the trail to migrate as far west as the Mississippi River. **Migrate** means to move from one region to another.

Revolutionary War

The **Revolutionary War** and the rush toward western settlement both began in 1775. Migration west, the mass movement of people, continued for years. The Wilderness Trail was improved and replaced in 1796 by a new wagon road to the Gap. This wagon road was one of the main routes used by settlers to reach Kentucky from the East. Over 300,000 settlers traveled along the Wilderness Road to the West from 1776 to 1810.

Migration & Immigration History Activities
Unit One: Settlement Beyond the Appalachian Mountains

Name: _____ Date: _____

Activity: Summarizing

Directions: Use information from the reading selection to complete the graphic organizer.

Push Factor

Push Factor

Push Factor

From 1776 to 1810, about 300,000 settlers migrated west over the Appalachian Mountains by way of the Wilderness Road.

Summary: _____

Pull Factor

Pull Factor

Pull Factor

Manifest Destiny

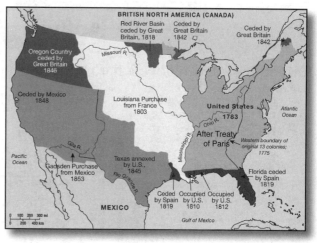

The United States population grew from more than five million in 1800 to more than 23 million by mid-century. This population explosion increased the need to expand into new territory. **Manifest Destiny** was the idea that the growth of the United States throughout the American continent was both a right and an obligation.

The United States Gains New Territory

As the country's third president, Thomas Jefferson doubled the size of the nation with the **Louisiana Purchase** from France in 1803. Eight present-day states were created in their entirety from the Purchase: Louisiana, Missouri, Arkansas, Iowa, North Dakota, South Dakota, Nebraska, and Oklahoma. The purchase also provided most of the land for the present-day states of Colorado, Kansas, Montana, Minnesota, and Wyoming.

James Polk became the eleventh president of the United States in 1844. In 1845, the Republic of Texas, which had broken away from Mexico while under the leadership of white settlers from the United States, was **annexed**, or joined with, the United States and became the 28th state.

The mountain region beyond the Louisiana Territory was known as the **Oregon Country**. During Polk's presidency, the **Oregon Treaty of 1846** was signed between the United States and Britain. The Treaty established the 49th parallel as the border of the United States and British-owned Canada. In 1848, Congress formally established the land as the **Oregon Territory**. The territory includes the present-day states of Washington, Oregon, and Idaho, and parts of Montana and Wyoming.

James Polk is best known for his territorial expansion of the nation through the Mexican American War of 1846. The **Treaty of Guadalupe Hidalgo** formally ended the war. The land **ceded**, or surrendered, to the United States by Mexico was referred to as the **Mexican Cession**. The territory was organized as California, Utah Territory, and New Mexico Territory, which includes the present-day states of California, Nevada, and Utah, most of Arizona, and parts of New Mexico, Colorado, and Wyoming.

Franklin Pierce was elected the 14th president of the United States in 1853. That same year, the United States paid Mexico $10 million for the **Gadsden Purchase**, a strip of land along the southern edge of the present-day states of Arizona and New Mexico. The purchase established the present-day Mexico-United States border.

Settlers Move West

As parts of the Louisiana Territory became settled, ordinary Americans began walking, riding, and driving wagons over the immense mountains to reach the fertile farmlands of Oregon Country and California. Some historians estimate that nearly 4,000,000 Americans moved to the western territories between 1820 and 1850.

Frontier land was usually inexpensive and sometimes even free, promising a better life for those who didn't own land. Some people moved west simply because they desired adventure. The discovery of gold in California in 1848 and the completion of the **Transcontinental Railroad** in 1869 were other factors that attracted people to the West.

Migration & Immigration History Activities Unit One: Manifest Destiny

Name: _____ Date: _____

Activity: Chronological Order

Directions: Use information from the reading selection to complete the timeline. Name the event(s) for each date.

Westward Growth of the United States During the 1800s

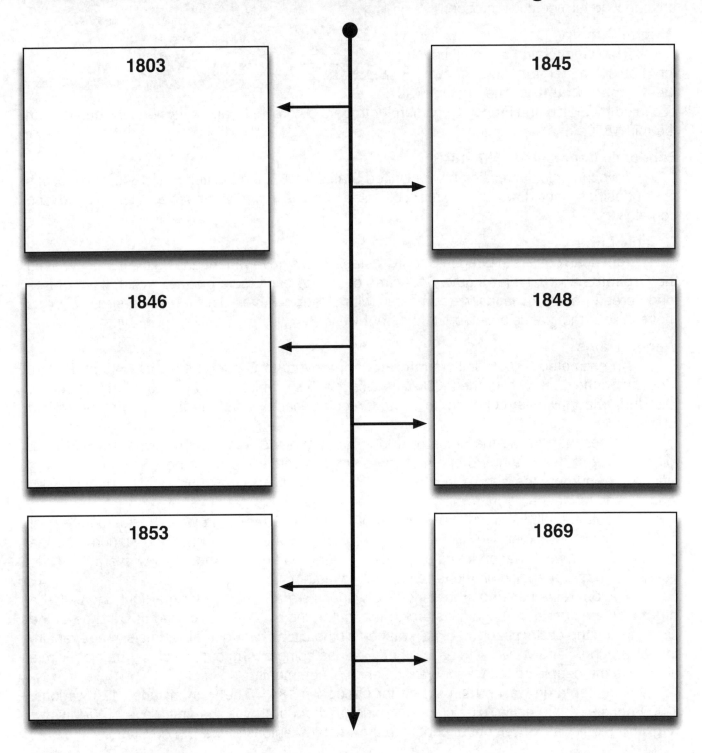

Oregon Fever

Mountain men and fur trappers were the first to use the route that became the Oregon Trail. Missionaries began traveling the trail to Oregon in the 1830s. Their letters home told of a land where anyone who farmed could prosper.

Oregon Country

The mountain region beyond the Louisiana Territory was known as the **Oregon Country**. The region was occupied by British and French Canadian fur traders before 1810 and by American settlers from the mid-1830s.

Economic Depression 1837–1843

An economic depression hit the United States in 1837 and lasted until 1843. Businesses and industries shut down and banks collapsed. People found themselves unemployed and homeless.

Organic Laws

American settlers in Oregon Country established a government and, in the 1840s, passed the **Organic Laws**. The laws gave 640 acres of land to each male pioneer. When word of free land spread east, thousands were infected with **Oregon Fever**. The term refers to the mass movement of thousands of settlers to the northwest.

Wagon Trains

An estimated 53,000 settlers **migrated**, or moved, to Oregon between 1840 and 1860. Most made the journey over the 2,000-mile **Oregon Trail**, which stretched from Independence, Missouri, to northwestern Oregon. In 1859, Oregon became a state in the union of the United States.

Rather than facing the perils of a long journey alone, most people who traveled west joined a **wagon train**, a group of ten or more wagons with 50 or more people led by a guide. During the journey, the people in a wagon train were like a small community. They elected leaders and made their own laws.

People traveled in many types of wagons, but the **Conestoga** was considered the best and was the most expensive. Horses, mules, or oxen were used to pull the wagons. As the groups traveled west, wagon trains stretched out for a half-mile or more. They averaged 12 to 15 miles a day, depending on the terrain and the weather.

Wagon trains halted before dark. The wagons were turned to form a tight ring called a **night circle** as protection against attack. Men took turns as sentries around the outside of the circle. Inside the circle, people cooked, washed clothes, took care of their animals, made repairs to their wagons, and visited with each other. Besides being a form of protection, the night circle also gave the people on the wagon train a sense of community.

The first large wagon train set off for Oregon in 1843. The train included 120 wagons, 1,000 people, 5,000 cattle, plus chickens, pigs, and dogs. It was the first wave of **Westward Migration**, or mass movement of people to the western regions of the United States.

Migration & Immigration History Activities — Unit One: Oregon Fever

Name: _____   Date: _____

Activity: Key Details

Directions: Use information from the reading selection to complete the page. Record key details about each topic. Use the details to write a summary.

Topic: Migration to Oregon Country

Push Factor: 1837 Economic Depression

Key Details

Pull Factor: 1840s Organic Laws

Key Details

Summary

The California Gold Rush

News of gold found at Sutter's Mill and other places in California caused one of the largest and wildest migrations in United States history. Between 75,000 to 100,000 people made their way to the California gold fields in 1849, hoping to become wealthy. Nicknamed **forty-niners**, most of the gold seekers were men. By 1859, women accounted for only eight percent of the population of California.

A woman with three men panning for gold during the California Gold Rush

John Sutter

When **John Sutter** arrived in California in 1839, that area was still part of Mexico. He convinced the Mexican government to give him 50,000 acres of land in the Sacramento Valley. Sutter built a fort of adobe bricks near where the American and Sacramento Rivers joined. After the Mexican American War ended in 1848, California became part of the United States.

Gold Discovered at Sutter's Mill

James Marshall, construction supervisor of a sawmill being built for John Sutter, was trying to solve problems that prevented the water from flowing forcefully enough to keep the waterwheel turning properly. On the morning of January 24, 1848, Marshall was checking the progress of the work when he noticed a few glittering flakes of gold. Returning quickly to the mill, Marshall shouted to the men, "Boys, ... I believe I have found a gold mine!"

Discovery Kept a Secret

When James Marshall brought him proof of the discovery of gold, Sutter asked Marshall to keep his discovery a secret. Marshall agreed. The workers also promised to keep the discovery secret until the mill was finished. However, a secret is difficult to keep, especially one as exciting as the discovery of gold. Even Sutter himself could not keep quiet. Within days of the discovery, he wrote in a letter: "I have made a discovery of a gold mine which, according to the experiments we have made, is extremely rich."

Sutter's secret made it to San Francisco as early as March 15, 1848. The news appeared as a small notice on the last page of the *Californian* newspaper. This announcement, however, didn't have much effect on the people of San Francisco.

Gold Fever

In May 1848, a man named Sam Brannan visited Sutter's Mill. Excited about finding gold, he returned to San Francisco. Waving a bottle of gold dust, he shouted, "Gold! Gold! Gold from the American River!" The news was like lighting a stick of dynamite; everyone exploded.

Gold fever, or a desire to find gold, struck immediately after Sam Brannan made his announcement. It infected tens of thousands of people. It affected people of every age, social class, and occupation: farmers, merchants, doctors, lawyers, rich men, and poor ones. Everyone with gold fever had one common goal—to cure the fever by searching for gold in California.

Migration & Immigration History Activities — Unit One: The California Gold Rush

Name: _____ Date: _____

Activity: Recalling Information

Directions: Use information from the reading selection to complete the graphic organizer.

California
- Sacramento River
- American River
- Sutter's Mill

Who were the 49ers?

What event caused the California Gold Rush?

Where in California was gold discovered?

When was gold discovered in California?

What were the push and pull factors for the California Gold Rush?

Homestead Act of 1862

In 1862, two years after the Civil War began, President Abraham Lincoln signed the **Homestead Act**. The law allowed any head of household who was a citizen or becoming a citizen, including formerly enslaved people and single women, to claim 160 acres of land for a small filing fee. All the settlers had to do was build a home, plant crops, and live on the land for five years.

Settlement of the Great Plains

The Civil War left thousands of farmers and formerly enslaved people homeless. Eastern farmland prices increased. The Homestead Act was designed to encourage settlement of the Great Plains region. The law made over 250 million acres of land open to homesteaders. Many people took advantage of the offer of free land and successfully **migrated**, or moved, to the Great Plains area. Kansas went from a population of 100,000 in 1860 to over 1 million in 1890; Nebraska from less than 30,000 to over 1,000,000; and North Dakota from less than 5,000 to over 300,000.

Life on the Great Plains

The **Great Plains region** was different from the area east of the Missouri River settlers left behind. It had little rainfall, and much of the moisture was lost by evaporation. Little rainfall, hot days, and high winds might destroy a ripening crop. Fierce winter blizzards, rains in the spring, and hot, dry summers made life miserable. Grasshoppers sometimes came in clouds that blotted out the sun and ate everything except metal when they landed.

The lack of trees made it difficult to supply wood for construction, fences, and firewood. The settlers could not build the usual home made of wood, so they dug a cave out of the side of a hill, dug a hole in the ground, or built a house called a **soddy** out of sod blocks. **Sod** refers to grass and the soil beneath it that is held together by the grass's roots. These types of homes could be built quickly. They were warm in the winter and cool in the summer, but a mouse or snake might drop in on the family dinner. A rain left drops of mud on the table and water pouring across the dirt floor. To heat the home, people burned hay and dry buffalo or cow manure.

New Inventions and Technology

Without technology, the region could have never developed as it did. Pre-Civil War inventions included **Cyrus McCormick's reaper**, invented in 1834, and **John Deere's steel plow** in 1837. After the Civil War, two new inventions were especially useful on the Great Plains. **Barbed wire** was invented in 1874 by **Joseph Glidden**, who twisted strands of wire with barbs at intervals. Fencing had never been possible on the Plains because of the lack of trees, but now it could be done at a reasonable expense. The more barbed wire that was produced, the less it cost. **Windmills** brought water from deep in the ground to the surface. They were too expensive for many farmers at first, but by the 1890s, windmills dotted the Plains.

Migration & Immigration History Activities Unit One: Homestead Act of 1862

Name: _____ Date: _____

Activity: Key Details

Directions: Use information from the reading selection to complete the graphic organizer.

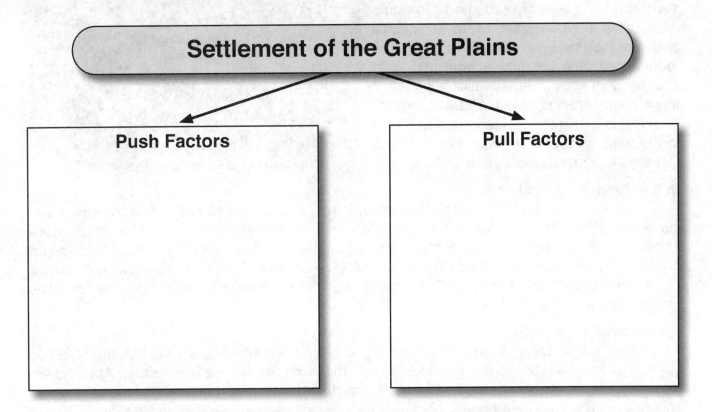

Settlement of the Great Plains

Push Factors

Pull Factors

Living in a Soddy	
Advantages	Disadvantages

Oklahoma Land Rush

In 1825, Congress set aside the land west of the Mississippi River as **Indian Territory.** Later laws in 1828 and 1834 would reduce the land to what would eventually become the state of Oklahoma. The law required all others to move from the area. The territory was over 40 million acres of fertile rolling prairies, rivers, and vast forests. Several Native American nations already lived in the area, including the Apache, Arapaho, Comanche, Kiowa, Osage, and Wichita.

The Oklahoma Land Rush begins, 1893.

Indian Removal Act of 1830

Under the terms of the **Indian Removal Act of 1830**, white settlers were required to leave the Indian Territory. More than 46,000 Native Americans east of the Mississippi were forced, sometimes by the United States military, to move from their ancestral lands to the Indian Territory. Among these were those known as the "Five Civilized Tribes": the Cherokee, Choctaw, Chickasaw, Creek, and Seminole. This removal was painful, and many died along the way. The journey came to be known as the "Trail of Tears."

Homestead Act of 1862

By the mid 1800s, much of the east coast of America was already settled. In 1862, two years after the Civil War began, President Abraham Lincoln signed the **Homestead Act**. The Act was designed to encourage settlement of the **western territories**, land west of the Mississippi River. The law allowed any head of household who was a citizen or becoming a citizen, including formerly enslaved people and single women, to claim 160 acres of land for a small filing fee. All the settlers had to do was build a home, plant crops, and live on the land for five years.

Economic Depression

The **Panic of 1893** was an economic depression in the United States that gripped the nation until 1897. Banks, railroads, and steel industries closed. Workers were laid off, and thousands became homeless.

Oklahoma Land Rushes

The Homestead Act of 1862 urged thousands of new settlers to **migrate**, or move, to the Great Plains with the offer of free land. The last part of the Plains to be settled was Oklahoma. President Benjamin Harrison had signed the **Indian Appropriation Act** in March 1889, opening the land to white settlers. When the first land rush took place on April 22, 1889, an estimated 50,000 settlers flooded into the region of central Oklahoma known as the **Unassigned Land** to claim land. A **land rush** is an event in which previously restricted land is opened to settlers on a first-arrival basis.

Other land rushes followed as more lands were opened to settlers. At twelve noon on September 16, 1893, a cannon boomed, beginning the largest land rush America ever saw. An estimated 100,000 people on horses, in wagons, or on foot raced to claim plots of land in the northern Oklahoma Territory known as the **Cherokee Outlet**.

Migration & Immigration History Activities

Unit One: Oklahoma Land Rush

Name:

Date:

Activity: Cause and Effect

Directions: Use the information from the reading selection to complete the graphic organizer.

The Oklahoma Land Rush

Cause

Effect

Homestead Act of 1862

Panic of 1893

Indian Appropriation Act of 1889

The Great Migration

A majority of African Americans in the United States lived in the South after the Civil War. To escape poor economic conditions and racial discrimination, African Americans moved north in large numbers from 1916 to 1930. **Racial discrimination** means the unfair treatment of someone or a group of people on the basis of their race.

African American families left the South in search of better economic and social opportunities in northern cities. The Arthur family arriving in Chicago, 1920.

After the Civil War

After the Civil War, most unskilled, formerly enslaved people resumed work on plantations as sharecroppers. The **sharecroppers** rented 10- to 50-acre plots. In exchange for land, a cabin, supplies, and a mule, sharecroppers agreed to raise a cash crop (usually cotton, tobacco, or rice) and give a portion of the crop to their landlord. After the harvest, the landlord paid the sharecropper a share of the profits from the crop, usually one-third to one-half. In this way, the landowners got workers without having to pay wages, and the sharecroppers got land to work without having to buy it. However, any debts or expenses encountered by the sharecropper had to be taken out of their share of the profits. Almost everything from food to shoes came from stores owned by the landlords. A year or two of bad crops could lead to the sharecroppers being hopelessly in debt to the landowner. In the 1890s and early 1900s, the boll weevil destroyed the cotton crop, causing an economic catastrophe and widespread unemployment in the South.

In 1865 and early 1866, the new southern state **legislatures**, or lawmaking bodies, passed a series of laws based on the **slave codes** that had been in effect since early colonial days restricting the behaviors of formerly enslaved people. The new laws were called Black Codes. **Black Codes** limited the civil rights of **freedmen**, formerly enslaved people. **Civil rights** are opportunities, treatment, and protection everyone is guaranteed under the law.

The Black Codes were designed to limit opportunities for freedmen. Unemployed and without a permanent residence, they could be declared **vagrants**. Vagrants were arrested and fined. If unable to pay, they were forced to work for white employers to pay off the fine. Black Codes also restricted freedmen from owning farms and certain businesses.

The Great Migration

After the Civil War, factories in northern cities needed workers. Freedmen were encouraged to move to these cities by African American newspapers such as the *Chicago Defender,* which featured advertisements for workers. With northern industries needing labor, African Americans moved north in large numbers from 1916 to 1930. The movement has become known as the **Great Migration**. During this time, over one million African Americans moved to northern cities such as New York, Philadelphia, Detroit, and Chicago. By the early 1900s, one-tenth of the African American population had moved to the North in search of better opportunities.

Name: _____ **Date:** _____

Activity: Word Meaning

Directions: Use information from the reading selection to complete the graphic organizer. Write a definition for each word and use it in a sentence.

Word Meaning		
Word	**What it Means**	**Sentence Using Word**
Racial discrimination		
Sharecropper		
Slave codes		
Black Codes		
Freedmen		
Civil rights		
Great Migration		

The Dust Bowl

The **Dust Bowl** was the name given to a drought-stricken region of the United States. This area suffered severe dust storms during a dry period in the 1930s. High winds and choking dust swept the region.

Farming and Living on the Great Plains
Life had always been difficult for homesteaders on the **Great Plains**, a large area of flatland across the Midwest. Before farmers moved to the area in the late 1800s, the land was covered with hardy grasses that held the fine-grained soil in place even during times of drought, wind, or torrential rains.

Farmer and his children walking in dust, 1936

When large numbers of homesteaders settled in the region in the late 1800s, they plowed up the grasses and planted crops. The cattle they raised ate whatever grass was left. This exposed the soil to the winds that constantly swept across the flat plains. When a series of droughts hit the area in the early 1930s, combined with the farming practices of the past 50 years, there was nothing to hold the soil in place.

The Dust Bowl
A large area in the southern part of the Great Plains region of the United States came to be known as the Dust Bowl during the 1930s when a ten-year drought hit the area. **Dust storms** swept the plains. Over time, as much as three to four inches of topsoil blew away, leaving only hard, red clay, which made farming impossible.

The windstorms carried walls of dust miles long and several thousand feet high across the plains, settling around homes, fences, and barns. People slept with wet cloths over their faces to filter out the dust. They woke to find themselves, their pillows, and blankets caked with dirt. Animals were buried alive or choked to death on the dust. Many people died from what came to be called **dust pneumonia**—severe damage to the lungs caused by breathing dust.

The Great Depression had already caused the price of wheat and corn to fall to all-time lows. When crops failed, farmers couldn't make mortgage payments on their farms. By 1932, a thousand families a week were losing their farms in Texas, Oklahoma, and Arkansas. Between 1930 and 1940, over 3 million people **migrated**, or moved, west in search of a better life.

End of Dust Bowl Era
In 1935, both the federal and state governments began developing programs to conserve the soil and reclaim the area. This included seeding large areas with grass, crop rotation, contour plowing, terracing, and strip planting. In some areas, "shelter belts" of trees were planted to break the force of the wind. In the fall of 1939, the rain finally returned in significant amounts to many areas of the Great Plains, signaling the end of the Dust Bowl.

Migration & Immigration History Activities

Unit One: The Dust Bowl

Name: Date:

Activity: Locating Information

Directions: Use the map to complete the activity.

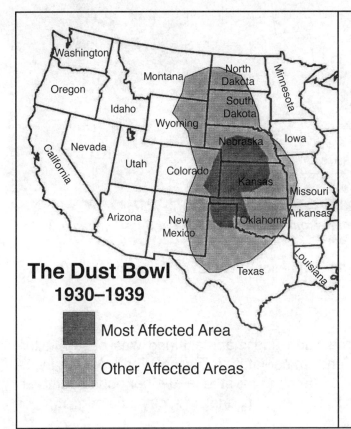

Name the states impacted by the Dust Bowl of 1930–1940.

1. _____
2. _____
3. _____
4. _____
5. _____
6. _____
7. _____
8. _____
9. _____
10. _____
11. _____
12. _____
13. _____

Directions: Use information from the reading selection to answer the questions below.

Question and Answers

1. What was the Dust Bowl?

2. What circumstances caused the Dust Bowl?

3. What were the effects of the Dust Bowl?

Recent Shifts in Population

Article One of the United States Constitution directs the population to be counted at least once every ten years. The **Census Bureau** is a government agency responsible for conducting the **census**, or count of the people. The first census was taken in 1790. At that time, the population of the United States was almost 4 million. The 2020 census showed that the total population of the United States is now over 300,000,000. The census also showed that as the population has grown, it has moved around a number of times during our history.

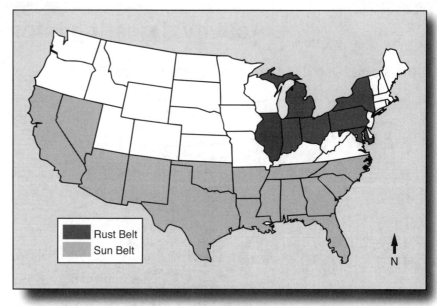

Population shifts from the Rust Belt to the Sun Belt began in the 1950s.

The Rust Belt

During the 1800s, most of the steel production and manufacturing was based in the northern states near the Great Lakes. During and immediately following World War II, these industries experienced a boom. With an increased demand for steel and other goods came an increased demand for workers. From the 1940s to 1960s, thousands of Americans **migrated**, or moved, to these industrial states looking for jobs.

By the 1970s, things started to change in the United States. People began relying on much cheaper foreign products. A decrease in demand caused the industries to shut down. The decline in the factories, the high unemployment, and the unused, rusting machinery left over from the industrial days earned the area the nickname **Rust Belt**. With the loss of economic opportunities in the northern states, people started moving in large numbers to other states to find work.

The Sun Belt

The **Sun Belt** is a region of the United States across the South and Southwest, characterized by a warm, sunny climate. The region includes 15 states: Alabama, Arizona, Arkansas, California, Florida, Georgia, Louisiana, Mississippi, Nevada, New Mexico, North Carolina, Oklahoma, South Carolina, Tennessee, and Texas. The Sun Belt has seen considerable population growth since the 1950s. In the 1950s, 28 percent of the national population lived in the southern states. Today, 40 percent of all the people in the United States live in the Sun Belt states. People migrate from the northern states to the southern states for several reasons, including the warm climate (made more bearable by the invention of air conditioning), retirement opportunities, and jobs linked to military bases, industries, agriculture, and commerical development. Federal civil rights and voting rights legislation in the 1960s also made the social and political climate more welcoming. The Sun Belt is still the fastest growing region of the United States.

Migration & Immigration History Activities

Unit One: Recent Shifts in Population

Name: _____ Date: _____

Activity: Textual Evidence

Directions: Use information from the reading selection to answer the questions below. Support your answers with specific details and examples.

1. What is the Census Bureau?

2. Why are the northern states near the Great Lakes referred to as the Rust Belt?

3. Why has the Sun Belt area of the United States experienced a population growth since the 1950s?

What Is Immigration?

The United States is often referred to as a "nation of immigrants." The Latin phrase *E Pluribus Unum* is usually found on the backs of American coins. The meaning of this phrase, "Out of many, one," reminds us that the United States is a nation made up of people with different backgrounds, beliefs, and cultures.

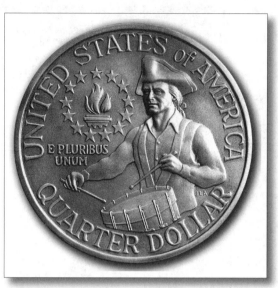

The Latin phrase "E pluribus Unum" is usually found on the backs of all American coins.

Types of Immigration

Immigration is the process of coming from another country to live permanently in a new country. The legal process for becoming an immigrant can be extensive. Those entering a country without meeting its legal requirements are sometimes called "undocumented immigrants."

The promise of a better life causes many immigrants to come to America. Many immigrants are refugees. **Refugees** flee to a new country to escape conditions such as war, persecution, or because their home government cannot protect them. Refugees must be approved before entering the United States. **Asylum seekers** are already in the United States or are at the border. They claim to be refugees, but their claims have yet to be evaluated. They must apply to stay in the country within one year of arriving. Whether a person is an immigrant, refugee, or asylum seeker, it can take years to get **legal status**, or the right to permanently live in the United States.

Push and Pull Factors

There are any number of reasons why people relocate from one country to a home in another country. These are referred to as push and pull factors. **Push factors** are conditions that "push" people away from their homes and include such things as too few jobs, wars, and natural disasters. **Pull factors** are conditions that "pull" people to a new home and include things such as jobs, higher wages, safety from violence, and the promise of a better life.

Immigration vs. Emigration

People move between countries or even parts of the world. Both immigration and emigration refer to this movement of people.
- **Immigration** is the process of <u>coming to</u> another country to live permanently. An **immigrant** is a person who comes to another country to live permanently.
- **Emigration** is the process of <u>exiting</u>, or leaving, one's country of origin to live in another country. An **emigrant** refers to an individual who exits their country of origin to live in another country.

A person can be an immigrant and an emigrant at the same time. For example, a person leaving Mexico to live permanently in the United States is an emigrant from Mexico. When that person moves into the United States, that person is considered an immigrant.

Migration & Immigration History Activities — Unit Two: What Is Immigration?

Name: _____ Date: _____

Activity: Word Meaning

Directions: Use information from the reading selection to complete the graphic organizer. Write a definition for each word.

1. legal immigrant	What's the difference?	undocumented immigrant

2. refugee	What's the difference?	asylum seeker

3. push factors	What's the difference?	pull factors

4. immigration	What's the difference?	emigration

5. immigrant	What's the difference?	emigrant

The Four Waves of Immigration

The history of immigration to the United States can be grouped into four major time periods or waves: Colonial Era 1607–1830, Mid-1800s, Turn of the 20th Century, Post-1965.

First Wave: The Colonial Era 1607–1830

The first wave arrived during the colonial period in the 17th and 18th centuries. This wave occurred mostly before the United States was founded and before official immigration records were kept. Though we do not know the exact numbers, this first wave consisted largely of people from Britain. Most people were looking for religious freedom and economic opportunity. These immigrants and their descendants eventually established the original Thirteen Colonies. Due to a labor shortage in the colonies, there were no restrictions or requirements for immigration. Among the early British settlers, up to 50,000 convicts were transported to the colonies from English jails. Also among this first wave were African immigrants. Unlike other immigrant groups, however, these people did not come willingly. Enslaved people from Africa were brought forcibly into the American colonies as early as 1619.

Second Wave: The Mid-1800s

The second wave of immigration did not occur until the mid-1800s. Following the American Revolution (1775–1783) hundreds of thousands of new immigrants came from Europe and Asia to the United States. Many Europeans were fleeing starvation in their homelands due to the Irish Potato Famine (1845–49) or the violence of the European revolutions of 1848. They were lured to the United States by the news of the discovery of gold in 1848 or the promise of free land offered by the Homestead Act of 1862. In 1882, due to the great number of immigrants coming to the United States during this wave, the government passed the first of several laws to restrict immigration.

Third Wave: The Turn of the 20th Century

The third wave of immigration to the United States occurred at the turn of the 20th century, around 1880 to 1914. Immigrants came from Southern and Eastern Europe (Italy, Russia, Austria-Hungary). The invention of large steam-powered oceangoing ships led to lower travel costs from Europe to the United States. The rapid rise in manufacturing in the United States increased demand for workers. Immigration slowed with the outbreak of World War I in 1914. In the 1920s, immigration was slowed again with the passing of new laws, setting **quotas**, or numerical limits, on the number of people who could enter the United States each year from Southern and Eastern Europe. Immigration slowed again during the Great Depression of the 1930s and World War II from 1939 to 1945.

Fourth Wave: Post-1965

The fourth wave of immigration started in 1965, with the largest immigrant groups coming from Asia, Latin America, and South America. Many of these immigrants left their home countries to escape dictatorships and civil wars. Some came to the United States in search of economic opportunity. A major difference between the Fourth Wave and earlier eras of immigration is the large group of illegal or undocumented immigrants. Many came over legally on temporary visas but stayed after the visas expired. A **visa** is a government-issued permit that allows an immigrant to legally enter the United States. Others walked in without visas, mostly over the Mexican border.

Migration & Immigration History Activities — Unit Two: The Four Waves of Immigration

Name: _____   Date: _____

Activity: Textual Evidence

Directions: Use information from the reading selection to answer the questions below. Support your answers with specific details and examples.

1. Characterize each of the "four waves" of immigration. When did it occur? Who were the primary immigrants, and where did they come from? What factors drove their immigration?

2. What caused the three lulls in immigration?

Colonial Era

The original 13 American colonies were a group of British settlements on the Atlantic coast of North America in the 17th and 18th centuries. In 1700, there were about 250,000 European settlers and enslaved Africans in the English colonies. By 1775, before the American Revolutionary War, the colonial population had grown to an estimated 2.5 million.

Thirteen Colonies

KEY
New England Colonies
Massachusetts, New Hampshire, Rhode Island, Connecticut

Middle Colonies
New York, New Jersey, Pennsylvania, Delaware

Southern Colonies
Maryland, Virginia, North Carolina, South Carolina, Georgia

Push and Pull Factors

The first wave of immigration was triggered by the discovery and exploration of the New World. The British expanded their empire by establishing the 13 colonies in the New World from 1607 to 1763. This presented many people with the opportunity to move to the colonies. The first groups came to escape religious persecution. From 1623 to 1624, crop failure and famine hit Northern England. Many people moved to the colonies to find more fertile land and to escape starvation. The introduction of the system of indentured servants enabled poor people to travel to the Americas. An **indentured servant** was a person who agreed to work for a person in the colonies in exchange for passage to the colonies. It allowed thousands to escape poverty and gain employment in the colonies. The English Civil War (1642–1651) brought conflict. Many fled to the colonies to escape the violence and an uncertain future.

Three British Colonial Regions

The American colonies were divided into three regions: the New England Colonies, the Middle Colonies, and the Southern Colonies. The colonies were made up of different pieces of land claimed by the monarchy of England.

The **New England Colonies** drew people from England, Ireland, and Scotland. The new colonies were dominated by the Puritans. They moved from England to practice their religion without persecution. The colonies were established to create wealth for England through trade. Most colonists worked in the fishing industry. Each colony was to send fish, whale products, and timber back to England in exchange for money, tools, and supplies they needed in the colony.

The **Middle Colonies** drew people from all over Europe. The ability to own land drew a variety of nationalities, including the Swedes, Germans, Dutch, and Irish. Religious tolerance attracted many religious groups such as Quakers, Catholics, Jews, Lutherans, and Presbyterians. The land and climate were good for farming. The Middle Colonies were called the "breadbasket colonies" because of the great amount of wheat grown in the region.

The **Southern Colonies** drew mostly English settlers. The colonists had a mixture of religions as well, including Baptists and **Anglicans** (members of the Church of England). The soil and climate of the Southern Colonies were excellent for crops like tobacco, rice, and **indigo** (a plant that produces a blue dye).

Migration & Immigration History Activities

Unit Two: Colonial Era

Name:

Date:

Activity: Compare and Contrast

Directions: Use information from the reading selection to complete the graphic organizer.

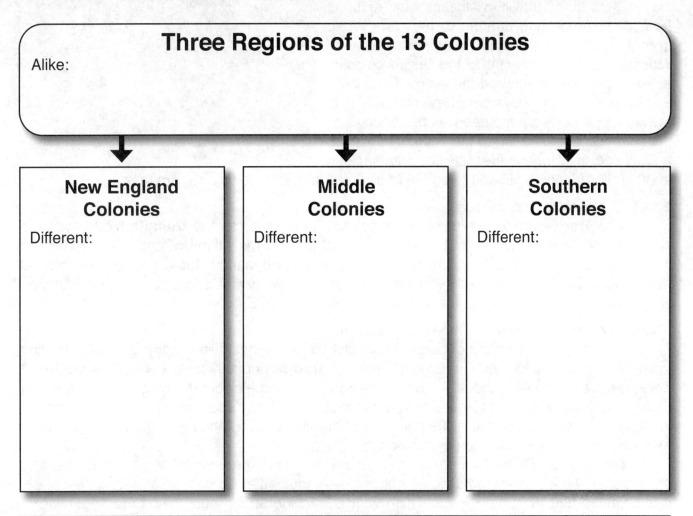

Three Regions of the 13 Colonies

Alike:

New England Colonies

Different:

Middle Colonies

Different:

Southern Colonies

Different:

Push and Pull Factors	
Push Factor from Europe	**Pull Factor to New World**
1. Discovery and Exploration of the New World	
2. British Establishment of the 13 Colonies	
3. Crop failure and famine hit Northern England	
4. Introduction of Indentured Servant System	
5. English Civil War	

Importation of Enslaved Africans

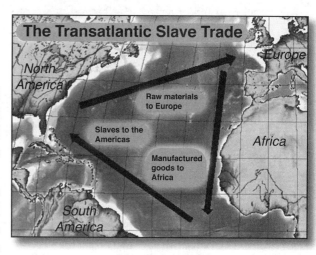

More than 12 million Africans were shipped from West Africa and brought to the New World from the 16th to the 19th centuries. Enslaved Africans were first brought to the British colonies as early as 1619. **Enslaved** means made a slave. Eventually, **slavery**, a system where one person is owned as property by another, was practiced in all the colonies. By 1776, when the Thirteen Colonies announced their independence from Britain, close to 300,000 Africans had been forced to **immigrate**, or move, to colonial America.

The Transatlantic Slave Trade

The **Transatlantic slave trade**, sometimes referred to as the **triangle trade**, was the selling of enslaved Africans by Europeans in and around the Atlantic Ocean. The triangular trade included three parts, in which arms, textiles, wine, and manufactured goods were shipped from Europe to Africa; enslaved people from Africa to the Americas; and sugar, tobacco, lumber, coffee, cotton, and other raw materials from the Americas to Europe.

The Beginning of Slavery in the British Colonies

The Virginia Company of London established the Jamestown Colony in 1607. The first indentured servants to arrive in Jamestown in 1609 were primarily from England. **Indentured servants** were people without enough money to pay for their ocean voyage. They signed a contract for free passage to America. The contract was sold to a farmer or merchant when the immigrant arrived, and in return, the person worked off the cost of the passage. It often took five to seven years of hard work to pay for the trip.

On August 20, 1619, a Dutch ship, the *White Lion,* brought 50 enslaved Africans to Jamestown. Twenty were sold as indentured servants. After their time of servitude ended, it is believed that they were freed. This event is considered by many to be the beginning of slavery in the British colonies in North America. However, the slave trade had been going on in the Caribbean, Central America, and South America almost from the beginning of European colonization. By 1675, African indentured servants in the colonies had become "servants for life" and then simply "slaves."

By the late 1600s, there were only 5,000 enslaved Africans in the 13 colonies. At this time, few came directly from Africa. Most were born in the colonies or had been shipped to the mainland from the West Indies. Several events occurred that increased the number of enslaved people. (1) The West Indies developed a surplus of slave labor, so farmers sold off unneeded workers at a reasonable price to farmers in the 13 colonies. (2) Rice and tobacco growers in the colonies needed many workers to produce the crops and could not find enough free laborers willing to work for low wages.

In the years that followed, many shiploads of Africans would arrive in North America, and those unwilling passengers would be sold. Colonists began to view enslaved workers as a less expensive, more plentiful labor source than indentured servants. Slavery was first recognized by Virginia law in the 1660s.

Migration & Immigration History Activities

Unit Two: Importation of Enslaved Africans

Name: Date:

Activity: Locating Information

Directions: Use information from the reading selection about slavery in the British colonies in North America to complete the graphic organizer.

The Irish Potato Famine

In the 1800s, Ireland was under the rule of Britain, and most of the land was owned by the British. Irish farmers rented the land from British landowners. Farmers paid the rent by selling the crops they grew and the animals they raised.

During the 1800s, anti-Irish feeling by many Americans grew.

A Time of Famine

By the late 1840s, many people across Ireland relied on potatoes as a vital part of their diet. Even though Ireland was known for producing livestock, dairy products, and some grains, most of the food was exported to England and other countries by the British landowners. Most Irish people grew potatoes for their own food and did not keep the other crops for themselves. From 1845 until 1852, Ireland experienced a time of famine known as the **Irish Potato Famine** or Great Irish Famine. It was a time when food was scarce, and many people died from starvation. The famine was caused by a disease called **potato blight**, a fungus that quickly destroyed the potato crops in Ireland. The effect was devastating for Ireland because potatoes were the staple food for most Irish people at the time.

Emigration

The famine caused widespread starvation, disease, and homelessness. It is not known exactly how many people died during the potato famine, but it is thought that around 1 million people lost their lives. Many people became homeless because they could not pay rent to their landlords. Many Irish families left the country and never returned. It is thought that as many as 2 million people **emigrated**, or moved out of a country, from Ireland to the United States and Britain from 1845 to 1855.

Irish Immigrants

Many Irish immigrants who reached America settled in Boston, New York, and other cities in the northeastern states. Almost all were poor and uneducated. Many spoke only the Irish language, called Gaelic, and could not understand English. To survive, they took work as laborers and servants.

Irish immigrants were not well-liked and were often treated badly. At this time, many Americans were unskilled workers and feared being put out of work by Irish immigrants willing to work for less than the going rate. The Irish also faced religious prejudice as almost all of them were Catholic. As anti-Irish and anti-Catholic sentiment grew, newspaper advertisements for jobs and housing routinely ended with the statement: "No Irish need apply."

Through the next decades, Irish workers contributed greatly to America's construction of canals, railways, and roads. Today, millions of people in the United States have a family connection with Ireland, even the 35th president. In 1960, John Fitzgerald Kennedy, the great-grandson of a potato famine immigrant, was elected president of the United States.

Migration & Immigration History Activities

Unit Two: The Irish Potato Famine

Name: Date:

Activity: Cause and Effect

Directions: Use information from the reading selection to complete the graphic organizer.

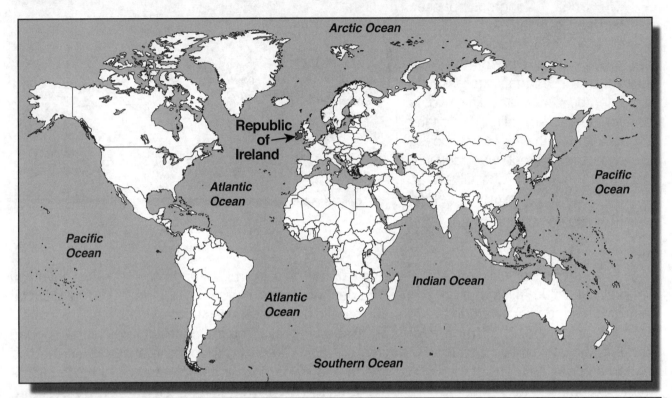

Irish Potato Famine

Date:

Define:

Cause	Effect

The Transcontinental Railroad

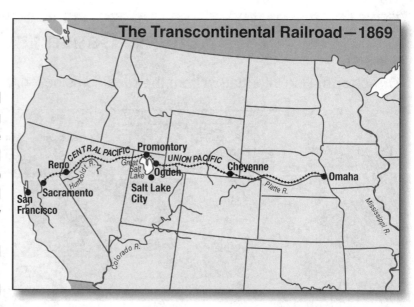

In 1862, Congress passed the **Pacific Railroad Act** providing federal land and funding for the construction of a **transcontinental railroad** from Omaha, Nebraska, to Sacramento, California. This would connect the eastern railroads already in operation with the west coast. However, the project was delayed until 1865 because of the Civil War. Chinese and Irish immigrants helped build the railroad.

Railroads

The project of building a continuous railroad line from California to Nebraska involved laying about 1,700 miles of track across prairies, deserts, mountains, and valleys. The **Central Pacific Railroad** was awarded the contract to build the line from California. It built approximately 690 miles of the line. The **Union Pacific Railroad** was awarded the contract to build the railroad from the Midwest. It laid about 1,085 miles of track. The federal government granted the two railroad companies loans of nearly $65 million and ownership of approximately 24 million acres of land to complete the project. On May 10, 1869, the two railroads met at **Promontory Summit, Utah**, where representatives of both railroads drove a golden spike to join the final rails.

Central Pacific Railroad

The Central Pacific Railroad started laying track in Sacramento, California, heading east in 1863. Soon, labor recruiters were scouring California, but the company struggled with hiring and retaining workers. The company began hiring Chinese immigrants who had arrived during the Gold Rush and advertised for more workers in China. China was facing many economic problems due to the **Opium Wars** (1850–1860) with Britain and France. The railroad was able to recruit over 10,000 Chinese men searching for employment and economic opportunities. From 1863 to 1865, the Chinese workers on the Central Pacific Railroad numbered about 15,000, or 80 percent of the entire workforce. The monthly wage for a Chinese worker averaged about $30.

Union Pacific Railroad

The Union Pacific Railroad began laying track in Omaha, Nebraska, heading west in 1865. The workforce included former soldiers from the North and the South, convicts from eastern prisons, as well as Mormons living near the railroad route in Utah Territory. By 1866, the railroad had also recruited approximately 10,000 Irishmen from eastern cities. The workers were drawn from the more than 1.5 million Irish immigrants who crossed the Atlantic to the United States from 1845 to 1855 to escape the **Irish Potato Famine**, a period of mass starvation and disease in Ireland. The monthly wage averaged about $45.

Migration & Immigration History Activities

Unit Two: The Transcontinental Railroad

Name: _____ Date: _____

Activity: Central Idea and Key Details

Directions: Use the information from the reading selection to complete the graphic organizer.

Central Idea: _____
_____

Central Pacific Railroad

Key Details:

Push and Pull Factors for the Chinese:

Union Pacific Railroad

Key Details:

Push and Pull Factors for the Irish:

The Chinese Exclusion Act

Americans encouraged immigration during the 18th and early-to-mid 19th centuries. As the number of immigrants rose in the late 1800s and an economic depression hit the United States, Congress began to pass legislation limiting Chinese immigration. Today, Chinese Americans make up the largest Asian population in the United States, totaling over 5 million.

Opium Wars

The first large wave of Chinese immigrants came to the United States in the 1850s, eager to escape the economic chaos caused by the **Opium Wars**, a conflict between China and two European countries: Britain and France. Many Chinese left the country and moved to the United States to find work.

A Chinese goldminer carries mining equipment on a shoulder yoke.

California Gold Rush

In 1848, gold was discovered in California. The discovery caused a **gold rush**, a rapid movement of people to the newly discovered goldfields. The news of the discovery attracted immigrants from around the world. By 1852, over 20,000 immigrants from China had arrived in America. As the goldfields became crowded and fewer people were discovering gold, anti-immigrant feelings soared.

When the Gold Rush ended in 1855, many Chinese miners took low-paying employment as farmhands, gardeners, and domestic help. Others created opportunities for themselves and started new businesses such as shops, restaurants, and laundries.

The Transcontinental Railroad

In the 1860s, it was Chinese immigrants who helped the Central Pacific Railroad build part of the **Transcontinental Railroad**. The company found it difficult to find workers, so they advertised for laborers in China. The railroad was able to recruit over 10,000 Chinese men searching for employment and economic opportunities. Chinese workers faced many challenges working on the railroad. They received lower wages than other workers for the same job. Often, they were given the most difficult and dangerous work, including digging tunnels and using explosives.

Chinese Exclusion Act

By the 1870s, resentment had grown toward the Chinese immigrants. There was an economic depression in America, and jobs became scarce. In 1880, President Rutherford B. Hayes signed a new treaty with China. The resulting **Angell Treaty** permitted the United States to restrict Chinese immigration. In 1882, Congress passed the **Chinese Exclusion Act**, banning Chinese immigration into the United States. The law was the first in American history to place broad restrictions on immigration. In 1943, when China became America's ally in World War II, Congress repealed the Exclusion Act.

Activity: Textual Evidence

Directions: Use the information from the reading selection to complete the graphic organizer. Support your answers with details and examples.

Event	Impact
Event 1 — Opium Wars	
Event 2 — California Gold Rush	
Event 3 — Transcontinental Railroad	
Event 4 — Chinese Exclusion Act	

World War I

When war broke out in Europe in 1914, nearly 15 percent of the people living in the United States were foreign-born immigrants. An **immigrant** is a person who comes to another country to live permanently. Most of those immigrants had come from European countries that would soon be involved in the war. Immigration rates to the United States decreased with the outbreak of World War I in 1914.

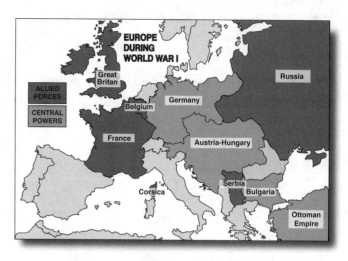

World War I

World War I began as a European war between Austria-Hungary and Serbia in 1914. It eventually grew into a war involving 32 countries. European countries began to form **alliances**, or defense agreements among nations. The major **Central Powers** included Germany, Austria-Hungary, and the Ottoman Empire. On the other side, the major **Allied Powers** included England, France, and Russia. Although the United States tried to remain neutral, it was drawn into the conflict in 1917, joining the Allied Powers.

One year after the war began, it had turned into a **stalemate**. Trenches were dug across northern France, and neither side could gain victory on the battlefield. Using a naval blockade, the British cut off German trade with neutral countries. The Germans countered using submarines known as **U-boats** to block supply lines to England.

In 1915, Germany used U-boats to sink the passenger ship *Lusitania*, killing more than 1,000 people, including 128 Americans. President Woodrow Wilson denounced the attacks, and Germany promised in the future to warn neutral ships before attacking. In 1917, President Wilson asked Congress to declare war on Germany after German U-boats attacked three American ships.

By 1918, the war was not going well for Germany. The German Army was running low on food and fuel. When it became apparent they were going to lose the war, the Germans signed an **armistice**, or agreement, ending the war on November 11, 1918. In January 1919, President Wilson and other world leaders met in Paris to negotiate a treaty ending the war. The **Treaty of Versailles** required Germany to make **reparations**, or payments, for the damage it had caused. The treaty also created new nations, including Czechoslovakia, Yugoslavia, and Poland.

Immigration

During the early years of the 20th century, an average of 1 million immigrants per year arrived in the United States. Up to this point, the United States had an **open-door immigration policy**, with no limit on the number of people who could enter the United States from Europe. Those arriving simply had to pass a medical and legal inspection.

The outbreak of World War I greatly reduced immigration from Europe. One reason was that transatlantic steamship travel became more limited and dangerous. Liners that had previously carried hundreds of immigrants were converted to wartime use, such as troop and cargo transports and as hospital ships. Those steamships that continued transporting immigrants to the United States were in danger of U-boat attacks similar to the attack on the *Lusitania* in 1915.

Migration & Immigration History Activities

Unit Two: World War I

Name: 	Date:

Activity: Textual Evidence

Directions: Use the reading selection to complete the graphic organizer. Support your answers with specific details and examples.

Who?

Who were the Allied Powers?

Who were the Central Powers?

Answer

When?

When was World War I?

Answer

Where?

Where was World War I?

Answer

What?

What effect did World War I have on immigration to the United States?

Answer

World War II

World War II (1939–1945) involved almost every nation in the world. Countries took sides and formed **alliances**, or defense agreements among nations. The **Axis Powers**, leaders of Germany, Italy, and Japan, worked together to control Europe and take over East Asia. Other nations sided with the **Allied Powers**, Great Britain, France, China, the Soviet Union, and the United States, as a defense against the attacks of the Axis Powers.

General of the Army Douglas MacArthur accepted the Japanese surrender.

Events of World War II

World War II began in September 1939, when Adolf Hitler, leader of the **Nazi Party**, or National Socialist Worker's Party, sent his armies into Poland. Two days later, Great Britain and France declared war on Germany. The following spring, France was invaded by Hitler's troops and surrendered a few weeks later. Then, in June 1941, Hitler attacked the Soviet Union. The United States was drawn into the conflict when the Empire of Japan attacked Pearl Harbor in Hawaii on December 7th.

After the attack on Pearl Harbor, many Americans worried Japanese Americans would side with Japan. In 1942, President Roosevelt signed Executive Order 9066, which ordered the evacuation of approximately 120,000 people of Japanese descent from the west coast to internment camps. An **internment camp** is a place where a government forces a large group of people to live. The Japanese Americans were held for up to four years before they were allowed to return home. By that time, many of their homes and businesses had been destroyed. In 1980, the government apologized, and the surviving Japanese Americans were each given a payment of $20,000.

In contrast, German and Italian non-citizens living in the United States only had to give up their weapons, shortwave radios, and maps and were put under travel restrictions. These restrictions were lifted in 1942. Only 15,000 Italians and Germans were ever interned.

The war in Europe finally ended on May 7, 1945, after Hitler had killed himself and the German High Command signed the surrender of all German forces.

The war with Japan continued until September 2, 1945. This was after President Harry Truman authorized dropping atomic bombs on two Japanese cities: **Hiroshima** and **Nagasaki**. An **atomic bomb** is a weapon of mass destruction that produces a massive explosion from a nuclear reaction. To prevent any further bombings, the Japanese surrendered.

Immigration

Tough immigration laws passed in the 1920s had limited the numbers of immigrants from Asia and Europe. Jews and other refugees who wanted to leave Germany and German-occupied territory found it almost impossible to get a visa to enter the United States. Immigration to the United States plummeted even further during World War II. After the war, people wanted to escape the devastation of the war-torn countries of Europe. At first, the United States refused to allow Jewish survivors of the Holocaust and other war refugees to immigrate. In June 1948, Congress voted to allow 200,000 displaced persons into the Untied States.

As the U.S. economy boomed after the war, there were jobs for nearly everyone who wanted one. Immigration began to increase again, and from the end of the war to 1950, over 1 million people had **immigrated**, or moved, to the United States, including over 200,000 from Germany, more than 100,000 from Great Britain, and close to 60,000 from Italy.

Migration & Immigration History Activities — Unit Two: World War II

Name: _____ Date: _____

Activity: Cause and Effect

Directions: Use information from the reading selection to complete the graphic organizer.

1. **Cause**

The Axis Powers worked together to control Europe and to take over East Asia.

→ **Effect**

2. **Cause**

After the attack on Pearl Harbor, many Americans worried Japanese Americans would side with the Japanese.

→ **Effect**

3. **Cause**

In August 1945, President Harry Truman authorized an atomic attack on Japan.

→ **Effect**

4. **Cause**

After World War II, refugees wanted to escape the devastation of war-torn Europe.

→ **Effect**

Immigration Laws

In the early years of the nation, there wasn't any such thing as "illegal" or "legal" immigration to the United States. The United States had an **open-door immigration policy**, with no limit on the number of people who could enter the United States. In the late 1800s, the first **laws**, or rules, were passed to regulate and restrict immigration to the United States.

THE AMERICANESE WALL, AS CONGRESSMAN BURNETT WOULD BUILD IT.
Uncle Sam: You're welcome in — if you can climb it!

Major Immigration Laws
- **1788** – The United States Constitution was officially ratified and became the highest form of law in the country. The Constitution gave the United States Congress authority over immigration.
- **1882** – The Chinese Exclusion Act banned the immigration of laborers from China for ten years because of anti-Chinese sentiment that developed during the Civil War era. Americans resented the Chinese immigrants because they were willing to work for lower wages. The Act was repealed in 1943 when China became an ally of the U.S. against Japan in World War II.
- **1891** – The Immigration Act appropriated money to build the first federal immigrant inspection station on Ellis Island on the east coast. European immigrants were subjected to medical and legal examinations during the inspection process.
- **1903** – Following the assassination of President McKinley in 1901 by the anarchist Leon Czolgosz, Congress enacted the Anarchist Exclusion Act, prohibiting the entry of people judged to be **anarchists**, people who rebel against authority, order, and the ruling power.
- **1917** – The Immigration Act of 1917 restricted immigration from Eastern Asia, except for Japan and the Philippines. The law also required a **literacy test**, or reading test, for all immigrants over 14 years of age.
- **1921** – The 1921 Emergency Quota Act limited the number of immigrants from certain countries after World War I.
- **1940** – The outbreak of World War II led to the Alien Registration Act that required the registration and fingerprinting of all **aliens**, or immigrants, in the United States over 14 years old.
- **1975** – The Indochina Migration and Refugee Assistance Act allowed Vietnamese, Cambodian, and Laotian people recruited by the United States in the Vietnam War to be admitted to the United States.
- **1986** – Immigration Reform and Control Act made it illegal to hire or recruit illegal immigrants.
- **1996** – Anti-terrorism and Effective Death Penalty Act tightened immigration to protect against terrorism following the attacks on Oklahoma City and the World Trade Center. **Terrorism** is the use of violence to achieve political goals.
- **2002** – The Enhanced Border Security and Visa Entry Reform Act were laws passed following the 9/11 terrorist attacks.
- **2006** – The Secure Fence Act authorized fencing along the U.S.-Mexican Border and the use of surveillance technology.

Migration & Immigration History Activities

Unit Three: Immigration Laws

Name: Date:

Activity: Locating Information

Directions: Use information from the reading selection to answer the questions.

Topic: Immigration Laws

1. What was the open-door policy?

2. What role does Congress play in immigration?

3. What is the purpose of immigration laws?

4. Why did the federal government establish Ellis Island as an immigration station?

The Statue of Liberty

The Statue of Liberty is considered a universal symbol of freedom. A **symbol** is something that stands for an idea. The statue has stood at the entrance of New York Harbor since 1886. For many years, it was one of the first glances of the United States for millions of immigrants from around the world.

A National Monument

The Statue of Liberty was given to the United States by the people of France, to represent the friendship between the two countries established during the American Revolution. It was designed by French sculptor Auguste Bartholdi. When the statue was completed in France in 1884, it was taken apart and shipped to the United States in crates and then rebuilt. On October 28, 1886, **President Grover Cleveland** dedicated the Statue of Liberty as a gift from the people of France.

The statue became a **national monument** and part of the National Park System in 1924. It is one of the most popular tourist destinations in the United States. Millions of tourists visit the monument each year. In 1984, the United Nations added it to the list of UNESCO World Heritage sites.

The Statue

The Statue of Liberty stands on **Liberty Island** in New York Harbor. The official name of the statue is *Liberty Enlightening the World*. The statue represents freedom and justice, basic ideas that shaped the creation of the United States.

Known as Lady Liberty, the monument is 305 feet high from the ground to the torch. The exterior of the statue is made of copper, which has turned green due to oxidation. The statue is the figure of a woman wearing a crown. She holds a torch in her raised right hand. The torch is a symbol of **enlightenment**, lighting the way to freedom. The seven rays in the crown represent the Earth's seven seas and seven continents. Visitors can climb the 377 steps to look out from one of the 25 windows in the crown. In her left hand, she holds a tablet. It represents the law. July 4, 1776, the date of the Declaration of Independence, is carved in Roman numerals on the tablet. The **stola**, or robe, is a symbol of the ancient Romans for freedom. The broken shackle and chain at the foot of the statue represent liberty breaking the chains of bondage. It commemorates the end of slavery in the United States.

The New Colossus

"The New Colossus" is a poem written by Emma Lazarus in 1883. Emma wrote the poem to raise money to construct a pedestal for the Statue of Liberty. In 1903, the poem was cast onto a bronze plaque and mounted inside the pedestal's lower level. Today, it resides in the Statue of Liberty Museum on Liberty Island.

> **The New Colossus**
>
> The last five lines of the poem read:
>
> "Give me your tired, your poor,
> Your huddled masses yearning to breathe free,
> The wretched refuse of your teeming shore.
> Send these, the homeless, tempest-tost to me,
> I lift my lamp beside the golden door!"

Migration & Immigration History Activities   Unit Three: The Statue of Liberty

Name: Date:

Activity: Locating Information

Directions: Use information from the reading selection to complete the graphic organizer.

Identify each part of the Statue of Liberty and what it symbolizes.

1.

2.

3.

4.

5.

Question and Answer

1. What is the Statue of Liberty's official title?

2. Who gifted the Statue of Liberty to the people of the United Sates?

3. Who wrote the poem that was placed on a plaque inside the pedestal's lower level?

4. Near which city is the Statue of Liberty located?

5. On which island is the Statue of Liberty located?

6. What does the Statue of Liberty symbolize?

Immigration Stations

Immigration refers to the process of coming to another country to live permanently. States controlled immigration until the late 1800s, and immigration to the United States was encouraged. The federal government assumed control of immigration in 1891. **Immigration stations** were established to hold, question, and check immigrants before being allowed to enter the United States.

Immigration Stations

By the early 1900s, many immigrants entered the United States through Ellis Island and Angel Island, the two largest immigration ports on either coast. Ships entering the harbors of the two cities would be met by immigration inspectors. The inspectors would board the ship and examine the passengers. Immigrants with the correct paperwork and free of diseases would be allowed to get off when the ship docked. Those who did not pass inspection were put on a ferry to the immigration station. Over 13 million people passed through the two stations.

Ellis Island Immigration Station

The **Immigration Act of 1891** funded the building of the first federal immigrant inspection station on Ellis Island in New York Harbor. The purpose of the station was to process immigrants to the United States from Europe. New York became known as the **Golden Door**, through which many immigrants to the United States passed.

Ellis Island operated from 1892 to 1954. The processing center began as a small island of only around 3 acres and grew to over 27 acres by 1906. It had its own power station, a hospital, laundry facilities, and cafeteria. Today, Ellis Island is part of the National Park System. Tourists can visit Ellis Island, where the main building is now an immigration museum.

Angel Island Immigration Station

Angel Island Immigration Station opened in 1910 and became the major port of entry to the United States for Asians and other immigrants coming to the west coast from the Far East. It was originally constructed to process Chinese immigrants whose entry was restricted by the **Chinese Exclusion Act of 1882**. Under the Chinese Exclusion Act, U.S. immigration officials were required to inspect each Chinese passenger who arrived by boat in San Francisco before they could enter the United States. The station included about 45 structures. There was

a hospital, a laboratory, barracks, a laundry, and a bathhouse. A fire led to its closure in 1940. In 1955, Angel Island was designated a California State Park.

Activity: Compare and Contrast

Directions: Use information from the reading selection to complete the graphic organizer.

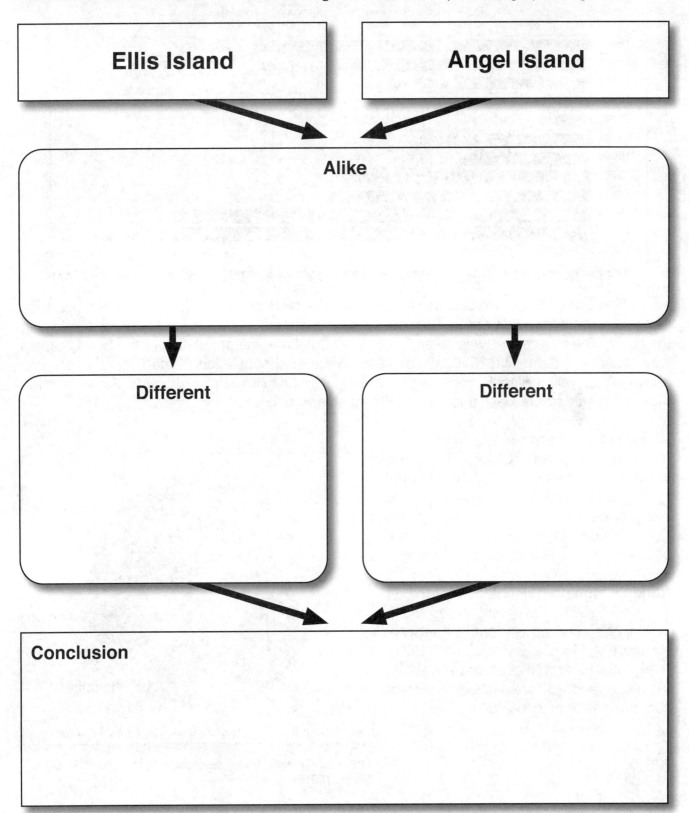

National Immigrant Heritage Month

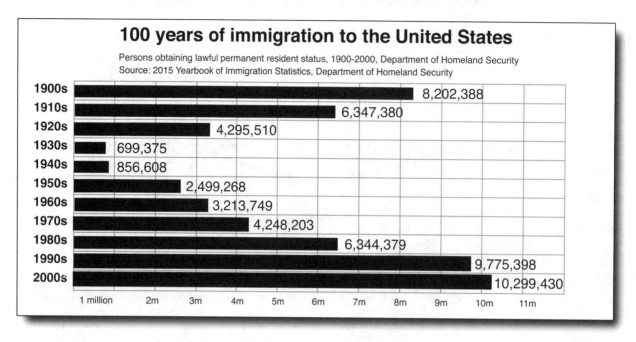

The United States Constitution requires a **census**, or count, every 10 years of all persons living in the country. The **Census Bureau** is the government agency responsible for conducting the count. The first census was taken in 1790. At that time, the population of the United States was almost 4 million. The 2020 census showed the total population of the United States has grown to over 300 million. Of the total population, over 40 million are immigrants. States with the most immigrants were California, Texas, Florida, New York, and New Jersey.

National Immigrants Day

The United States Congress designated October 28, 1987, as **National Immigrants Day**. President Ronald Reagan called upon the people of the United States to observe that day with programs, ceremonies, and activities.

National Immigrant Heritage Month

In 2021, President Joe Biden proclaimed June as **National Immigrant Heritage Month**. President Biden designated the month as a time to celebrate the history and achievements of immigrant communities across the country.

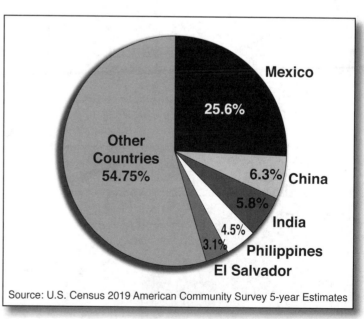

The five largest immigrant populations in the United States (2019)

Activity: Drawing a Conclusion

Directions: Study the map below. What conclusion can you draw about the immigrant population in 2018?

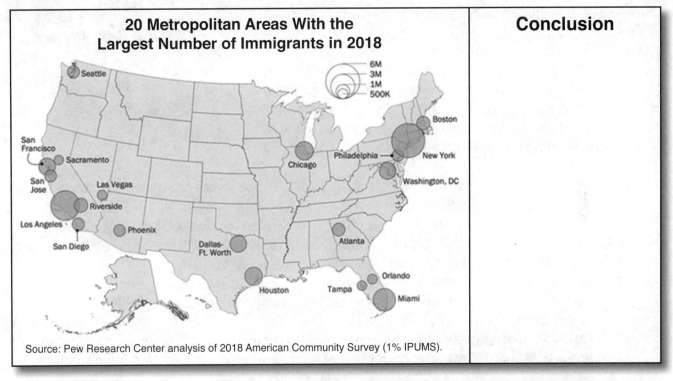

Directions: Think about what you learned from the reading selection. Study the pie chart below. What can you conclude about the importance of National Immigrant Heritage Month to Americans?

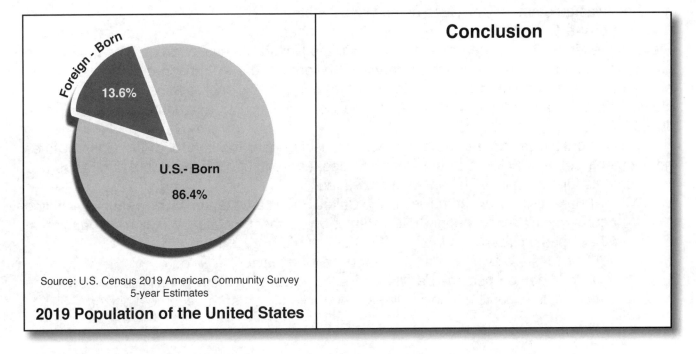

The Constitution and Citizenship

A **citizen** is a person who is recognized as a legal member of a country. The United States Constitution, along with the 27 Amendments, define our government and guarantee our rights as citizens.

The United States Constitution

The Constitution was signed on September 17, 1787. The Bill of Rights (first ten amendments) was **ratified**, or approved, on December 15, 1791. Three fundamental concepts about United States citizenship are found in those documents. However, they did not define citizenship.

1. *jus soli*: the right of the soil, which means that those born on United States soil are automatically granted citizenship.
2. **Naturalization**: is the process of becoming a United States citizen if a person was born outside of the United States. Naturalized citizens have the same privileges and responsibilities as U.S.-born citizens, including the right to vote.
3. **Rights of Citizens**: All citizens are guaranteed the right to "equal protection of the laws."
   - No state can make or enforce laws that take away the rights and privileges of citizens of the United States.
   - No state can take away from any person their life, liberty, or property without fair processes, nor deny equal protection of the law to anyone within its boundaries.

The Fourteenth Amendment

Prior to the Civil War, both state and national citizenship were the subjects of considerable debate. Each state had the right to determine citizenship, and anyone who became a citizen of any state was automatically a citizen of the United States.

After the Civil War, views on citizenship changed. In 1866, Representative Thaddeus Stevens presented the Fourteenth Amendment to the United States Congress. The goal was to protect the rights of formerly enslaved people. President Andrew Johnson did not support the amendment. Johnson **vetoed** it, or refused to sign it into law. Congress successfully overrode his veto, and the amendment was added to the Constitution. The amendment was ratified on July 9, 1868.

The **Fourteenth Amendment** placed citizenship under the control of the United States government, defined a citizen of the United States, and established the rights of citizens and requirements for citizenship. The amendment stated
- All persons born or naturalized in the United States are granted **citizenship**—including formerly enslaved people. **Naturalization** is the process by which an immigrant becomes a citizen.
- All citizens are awarded "equal protection of the laws."
- Once a person becomes a United States citizen, their citizenship cannot be taken away. The exception to this is if that person lied in order to become a citizen.

Migration & Immigration History Activities Unit Four: The Constitution and Citizenship

Name: _____ Date: _____

Activity: Locating Information

Directions: Use information from the reading selection to complete the page.

Multiple Choice

1. Which conflict led to the Fourteenth Amendment?
   A. The Revolutionary War
   B. The Civil War
   C. World War I
   D. World War II

2. The Fourteenth Amendment was initially put into place to protect what group of people?
   A. formerly enslaved people
   B. former slave owners
   C. members of Congress
   D. plantation owners

3. To become a citizen of the United States, a person must
   A. have a grandparent who was born in the United States.
   B. have been born in the United States.
   C. have cousins who are citizens of the United States.
   D. have been born or naturalized in the United States.

Fill in the Blanks

4. Naturalization is _____
   _____.

5. A citizen is _____
   _____.

6. The Fourteenth Amendment was ratified on July 9, _____.

7. Explain the importance of the Fourteenth Amendment.

Naturalization

Throughout the history of the United States, many people have **immigrated**, or moved, to the United States from other countries. Immigrants can become citizens of the United States. Over 600,000 immigrants become United States citizens each year.

United States Citizenship

A **citizen** is a person who is recognized as a legal member of a country. Citizens of the United States have certain rights. They can vote in elections, run for public office, work for the government, and are protected by United States laws. A person can become a United States citizen by birth or through naturalization.

- **Native citizen**: a person born in the United States is automatically considered a citizen of the country. This also includes people born outside the United States to a parent or parents who are U.S. citizens.
- **Naturalized citizen**: a person who immigrates to the United States and then becomes a citizen.

Immigrants

Many people in the United States have come here from other countries. Those who have not become citizens are referred to as **aliens**, or noncitizens. Some aliens come to the United States for a short period of time as tourists or students. Others come as immigrants. All aliens must apply to the United States government for permission to come to the country. Students and visitors receive a **visa** when their application is approved. An immigrant receives a **Green Card** when their application is approved. The Green Card entitles the person to permanently live and work in the United States.

Naturalization Process

The process by which immigrants become citizens is called **naturalization**. To qualify for naturalization, immigrants must be 18 years old, have demonstrated good moral character, be able to speak and understand English, and be willing to take an oath of loyalty to the United States. There are several steps in the process.

- **Application**: The person must fill out an application and send this to the **United States Citizenship and Immigration Services** for processing.
- **Fingerprinting**: The FBI fingerprints the person and does a background check to make sure they have not committed any major crimes.
- **Interview**: An immigration officer asks the person questions about their job, home, family, and background. They are tested on their ability to read and write English. They are questioned about the history and government of the United States.
- **Oath**: The final step in becoming a United States citizen is taking the **Oath of Allegiance**. The oath is a promise to obey the laws of the Constitution and to defend the United States.

Once an immigrant has completed the steps in the naturalization process and taken the oath, they receive a **Certificate of Naturalization** and are officially a U.S. citizen. The document proves the person obtained citizenship through naturalization. If the immigrant has children under 18, those children automatically become naturalized and can get a Certificate of Naturalization.

Migration & Immigration History Activities — Unit Four: Naturalization

Name: Date:

Activity: Word Meaning

Directions: Use the information from the reading selection to complete the graphic organizer. Write a definition for each word.

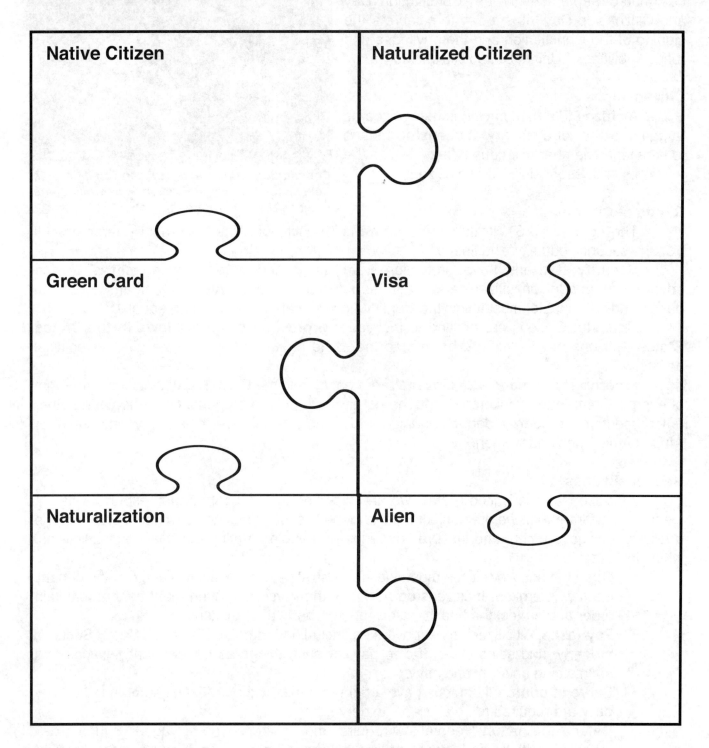

Rights and Responsibilities of Citizenship

The United States Constitution was signed on September 17, 1787. In 2004, Congress designated September 17 as "Constitution Day and Citizenship Day." It is a day to celebrate the signing of the Constitution and the privileges and responsibilities of United States citizenship.

Citizenship

A **citizen** is a person who is recognized as a legal member of a country. **Citizenship** means to be a legal member of a country and to have the full rights and responsibilities of a citizen.

Constitution Day and Citizenship Day is September 17. Naturalization ceremonies are often held on or around this date.

Rights of Citizens

The rights of U.S. citizens come from the Constitution. The document guarantees all citizens security, equality, and liberty.

Security: Citizens have protection from unfair and unreasonable actions by the government. In addition, citizens are guaranteed **due process of law**, which means laws must be fair and reasonable, must follow the Constitution, and apply to everyone equally.

Equality: Citizens are entitled to the **equal protection of all the laws in the United States**. Citizens have a right to be treated the same regardless of race, religion, or political beliefs.

Liberty: The **freedoms of citizens** are presented in the Bill of Rights, including freedom of expression, freedom of worship, and the right to own private property. Over the years, other amendments have been added, extending certain rights of citizens, including voting rights for African Americans and women.

Responsibilities

As citizens of the United States, we are expected to carry out certain responsibilities. If we fail to perform them, we are subject to legal penalties, such as fines and imprisonment. The quality of our government and our lives depends on people carrying out their responsibilities, which include:

- **Obey laws**: Every citizen must obey federal, state, and local laws and pay the penalty if a law is broken. If citizens do not obey the laws, the government cannot maintain order and protect the health, safety, and property of all citizens.
- **Pay taxes**: All citizens must pay taxes, including federal, state, local, Social Security, property, and sales taxes. Taxes pay for such things as government services and maintaining an army and navy.
- **Serve in court**: All persons have a right to a trial by jury. Citizens summoned to **jury duty** are required to be available to serve.
- **Defend the nation**: Federal law requires male citizens who are aged 18 through 25 to register with the **Selective Service**, an agency responsible for running the **draft**, or process for calling up people for military service in case of a national emergency.

Migration & Immigration History Activities

Unit Four: Rights and Responsibilities of Citizenship

Name: _____   Date: _____

Activity: Key Details

Directions: Use information from the reading selection to complete the graphic organizer.

United States Citizenship

Citizenship

Definition:

↙ ↘

Rights

Responsibilities

Answer Keys

Note: Some answers may vary. Suggested answers are given, but students may have other valid answers. Teacher check for appropriate responses.

Unit One: Major Migration Events
What Is Migration: Word Meaning (p. 3)
Migration: the mass movement of a population within a country or region
Immigration: refers to the process of moving to another country to live permanently
Push Factors: conditions that "push" people away from their homes and include such things as too few jobs, low wages, and natural disasters
Pull Factors: conditions that "pull" people to a new home include things such as safety, jobs, higher wages, and the promise of a better life

Prehistoric Migration to the Americas: Summarizing (p. 5)
Key Details
1. The last Ice Age created the Bering Land Bridge.
2. Prehistoric people followed animals from Asia to North America.
3. Early people migrated throughout North and South America.

Summary
   The prehistoric migration to the Americas began during the last Ice Age. The first people to arrive in North America followed the grass-eating animals across the Bering land bridge from Asia during this time. Following the migrating herds, they finally spread out and moved to the eastern parts of North America. In time, these people migrated as far south as the tip of South America. These early people were the ancestors of the Native Americans or First Nations peoples.

The Industrial Revolution: Word Meaning (p. 7)
Definitions
Industrial Revolution: the time in history when the production of goods moved from small shops and homes to large factories using power-driven machinery
Migration: the mass movement of people from one region to another
Urbanization: the migration of people from rural to urban areas
Migration From Rural to Urban Areas–Push: people who had worked on a farm migrated to cities to work in factories
Migration From Rural to Urban Areas–Pull: demand for labor and paying jobs

Settlement Beyond the Appalachian Mountains: Summarizing (p. 9)
Push Factors: overcrowding in colonies, colonists desired new land to settle, the Revolutionary War
Pull Factors: fertile lands between the Appalachian Mountains and the Mississippi River, Cumberland Gap discovered, Wilderness Trail cut through the Appalachians
Summary
   From 1776 to 1810, about 300,000 settlers migrated west over the Appalachian Mountains. Several conditions pushed the colonists from their homes and pulled them westward. Over 2 million people lived in the 13 colonies. Many believed it was too crowded and began looking for new land to settle. In 1775, the American Revolution began, and people wished to escape the war. The Cumberland Gap, a pass through the Appalachian Mountains that had been used by Native Americans, was discovered by Dr. Thomas Walker. In 1775, Daniel Boone created the Wilderness Trail through the Appalachian Mountains into the fertile lands between the Appalachians and the Mississippi River. Thousands of pioneers used the trail to migrate west.

Manifest Destiny: Chronological Order (p. 11)
1803: Louisiana Purchase
1845: Texas was annexed and became a state
1846: Oregon Treaty
1848: Congress established Oregon Territory, Mexican Cession
1853: Gadsden Purchase
1869: Transcontinental Railroad completed

Oregon Fever: Key Details (p. 13)
Push Factors: economic depression from 1837 to 1843; businesses and industries shut down and banks collapsed; people unemployed and homeless
Pull Factors: Oregon Country passed the Organic Laws; gave 640 acres of land to each male pioneer
Summary
   An estimated 53,000 settlers migrated to Oregon between 1840 and 1860. An economic depression hit the United States in 1837 and lasted until 1843. Businesses and industries shut down and banks collapsed. People found themselves unemployed and homeless. During this time, American settlers in Oregon Country established a government and passed the Organic Laws. The laws gave 640 acres of land to each male pioneer. When word of free land spread east, thousands were infected with Oregon Fever.

The California Gold Rush: Locating Information (p. 15)

Who?: a person who migrated to California in the year 1849 to search for gold
What?: gold found by James W. Marshall at Sutter's Mill
Where?: Sutter's Mill on the American River in California
When?: January 24, 1848
Push Factors: Gold Fever, people were infected with Gold Fever, desire to cure Gold Fever by discovering gold in California
Pull Factors: gold discovered in California, hope of becoming wealthy

Homestead Act of 1862: Key Details (p. 17)

Settlement of the Great Plains
Push Factors: The Civil War had left thousands of farmers and formerly enslaved people homeless. Eastern farmland prices increased.
Pull Factors: Homestead Act 1862, offer of free land
Advantages: They did not need wood to build a soddy. Soddies could be built quickly. They were warm in the winter and cool in the summer.
Disadvantages: A mouse or snake might drop in on the family dinner. A rain left drops of mud on the table and water pouring across the dirt floor.

Oklahoma Land Rush: Cause and Effect (p. 19)

Homestead Act of 1862
Effect: The Homestead Act of 1862 urged thousands of new settlers to migrate to the Great Plains with the offer of free land.
Panic of 1893
Effect: Banks, railroads, and steel industries closed. Workers were laid off, and thousands became homeless.
Indian Appropriation Act of 1889
Effect: An estimated 50,000 people flooded into the region of central Oklahoma known as the Unassigned Land.

The Great Migration: Word Meaning (p. 21)

racial discrimination: unfair treatment against someone or a group of people on the basis of their race
sharecropper: a person who agreed to raise a cash crop and give a portion of the crop to their landlord
slave codes: laws since early colonial days, restricting the behaviors of enslaved people
Black Codes: Black Codes limited the civil rights of freedmen
freedmen: formally enslaved people
civil rights: opportunities, treatment, and protection everyone is guaranteed under the law
Great Migration: the movement of large numbers of African Americans north from 1916 to 1930

The Dust Bowl: Locating Information (p. 23)

The Dust Bowl (States may be listed in any order.)
1. Montana
2. Wyoming
3. Colorado
4. New Mexico
5. North Dakota
6. South Dakota
7. Nebraska
8. Kansas
9. Oklahoma
10. Texas
11. Iowa
12. Missouri
13. Arkansas

Questions and Answers
1. The Dust Bowl was the name given to a drought-stricken region of the United States during the 1930s that suffered from severe dust storm.
2. The Dust Bowl was caused by severe dust storms during a dry period in the 1930s. Farming and overgrazing had exposed the soil to wind erosion.
3. Topsoil blew away, leaving only hard, red clay, which made farming impossible. Windstorms carried walls of dust miles long and several thousand feet high across the plains, settling around homes, fences, and barns. People slept with wet cloths over their faces to filter out the dust. Animals were buried alive or choked to death on the dust. Many people died from dust pneumonia. Between 1930 and 1940, over 3 million migrated west in search of a better life.

Recent Shifts in Population: Textual Evidence (p. 25)

1. Article One of the Constitution directs the U. S. population be counted at least once every ten years. The Census Bureau is a government agency responsible for conducting the census, or count, of the population.
2. During the 1800s, most of the steel production and manufacturing was based in the northern states near the Great Lakes. By the 1970s people began relying on much cheaper foreign products. Decrease in demand caused the industries to shut down. The unused machinery left over from the industrial days earned the area the nickname, Rust Belt.
3. The Sun Belt is a region across the South and Southwest, characterized by a warm, sunny climate. People migrate to states in these areas for several reasons including the warm climate, retirement opportunities, and availability of jobs linked to military bases, industries, agriculture, and commercial development. After civil and voting rights legislation, the South became more socially and politically welcoming.

Migration & Immigration History Activities — Answer Keys

Unit Two: Major Immigration Events
What Is Immigration: Word Meaning (p. 27)
1. A legal immigrant is a person who has met the legal requirements to enter another country to establish residency. An undocumented immigrant is a person who enters a country without meeting the legal requirements for entry.
2. A refugee is an immigrant who must be approved before traveling to the United States. An asylum seeker is an immigrant who is already in the United States or at the border waiting to be approved to stay in the country.
3. Push factors are conditions that "push" people away from their home. Pull factors are conditions that "pull" people to a new home.
4. Immigration is the process of <u>coming to</u> another country to live permanently. Emigration is the process of <u>exiting</u>, or leaving, one's country of origin to live permanently in another country.
5. An immigrant is a person who comes to another country to live permanently. An emigrant is a person who leaves their country of origin to live permanently in another country.

The Four Waves of Immigration: Textual Evidence (p. 29)
1. <u>First Wave</u>
   When?–Colonial Period 1607–1830
   Who?–British and African
   What?–religious freedom, economic opportunity
   <u>Second Wave</u>
   When?–Mid-1800s
   Who?–European and Asian
   What?–Irish Potato Famine (1845–49), European revolutions of 1848
   What?–discovery of gold in 1848, Homestead Act of 1862
   <u>Third Wave</u>
   When?–Turn of the 20th Century
   Who?–Southern and Eastern Europe (Italy, Russia, Austria-Hungary)
   What?–rapid rise of manufacturing in the United States, increased demand for workers
   <u>Fourth Wave</u>
   When?–Post-1965
   Who?–Asia and Latin America and South America
   What?–to escape dictatorships and civil wars, economic opportunity
2. World War I 1914–1918, the Great Depression of the 1930s, and World War II from 1939–1945

Colonial Era: Compare and Contrast (p. 31)
<u>Alike</u>: The 13 Colonies were British settlements on the Atlantic coast of North America.
<u>New England Colonies</u>: Colonists were from England, Ireland, and Scotland. Puritans wanted to escape religious persecution. Fishing main industry.
<u>Middle Colonies</u>: The ability to own land drew a variety of nationalities including the Swedes, Germans, Dutch, and Irish. Religious tolerance attracted many religious groups such as Quakers, Catholics, Jews, Lutherans, and Presbyterians. Religious tolerance. They were called the "breadbasket colonies" because the land and climate were good for growing wheat.
<u>Southern Colonies</u>: The colonies drew mostly English settlers. The colonists had a mixture of religions as well, including Baptists and Anglicans (members of the Church of England). The soil and climate were excellent for crops like tobacco, rice, and indigo.
1. opportunity for the British to expand their empire
2. opportunity to escape religious persecution
3. fertile land in the colonies
4. opportunity for a poor person to get to the New World
5. opportunity to escape violence of war

Importation of Enslaved Africans: Locating Information (p. 33)
<u>What?</u>: Slavery is a system where one person is owned as property by another.
<u>How?</u>: The first African-born "servants" arrived from the West Indies in 1619 and were listed as indentured servants.
<u>Why?</u>: Colonies needed many workers to produce the crops and could not find enough free laborers willing to work for low wages.
<u>Where?</u>: Jamestown, Virginia
<u>When?</u>: 1619

The Irish Potato Famine: Cause and Effect (p. 35)
Irish Potato Famine
<u>Date</u>: 1845–1852
<u>Define</u>: It was a time in Ireland when food was scarce and many people died from starvation.
<u>Cause</u>: The famine was caused by a disease called potato blight, a fungus that quickly destroyed the potato crops in Ireland.
<u>Effect</u>: The famine caused widespread starvation, disease, and homelessness. Many Irish families left the country and never returned. It is thought that as many as 2 million people emigrated from Ireland to the United States and Britain.

The Transcontinental Railroad: Central Idea and Key Details (p. 37)
Central Idea: Many Chinese and Irish immigrants helped build the Transcontinental Railroad from Omaha, Nebraska, to Sacramento, California.
Central Pacific Railroad
Key Details: The Central Pacific Railroad started in Sacramento, California, heading east in 1863. The company struggled with hiring and retaining workers. The company hired Chinese immigrants who had arrived during the Gold Rush and advertised for workers in China. The railroad was able to recruit over 10,000 workers from China.
Push and Pull: Push–China was facing many economic problems due to the Opium Wars. Pull–The Central Pacific Railroad Company advertised for workers in China. $30 monthly wage
Union Pacific Railroad
Key Details: The Union Pacific Railroad began in Omaha, Nebraska, heading west. The workforce included former soldiers, convicts, Mormons living near the railroad route in Utah Territory, and Irishmen. By 1866, the railroad had recruited approximately 10,000 Irishmen from eastern cities.
Push and Pull: Push–Irish Potato Famine. Pull–Jobs; $45 monthly wage

The Chinese Exclusion Act: Textual Evidence (p. 39)
Event 1: Opium Wars caused economic chaos in China. Many Chinese moved to the United States to find work.
Event 2: Over 20,000 Chinese immigrants moved to America.
Event 3: 10,000 Chinese men searching for employment and economic opportunities immigrated to the United States to work building the railroad.
Event 4: The law banned Chinese immigration into the United States.

World War I: Textual Evidence (p. 41)
Who?: Allied Powers included England, France, Russia, and the United States. Central Powers included Germany, Austria-Hungary, and Ottoman Empire.
When?: 1914–1918
Where?: mostly in Europe
What?: reduced immigration from Europe

World War II: Cause and Effect (p. 43)
1. World War II began
2. Japanese Americans had to leave their homes along the west coast and go to internment camps.
3. Two atomic bombs were dropped on Japan. Japan agreed to surrender. September 2, 1945, Japan signed an agreement of peace.
4. At first, the United States refused to allow Jewish survivors and other refugees to immigrate, but Congress allowed 200,000 displaced persons to immigrate in 1948. After the war by 1950, over 1 million people had immigrated to the United States, including over 200,000 from Germany, more than 100,000 from Great Britain, and close to 60,000 from Italy.

Unit Three: Coming to America
Immigration Laws: Locating Information (p. 45)
1. no limit on the number of immigrants who could enter the United States
2. has authority over immigration
3. to regulate and restrict immigration
4. to examine immigrants before allowing them to enter the United States

The Statue of Liberty: Locating Information (p. 47)
Statue of Liberty
1. torch–a symbol of enlightenment
2. crown and seven rays–the Earth's seven seas and seven continents
3. tablet–law
4. stola–freedom
5. broken shackle and chain–liberty breaking the chains of bondage; end of slavery in United States

Question and Answer
1. Liberty Enlightening the World
2. people of France
3. Emma Lazarus
4. New York City
5. Liberty Island
6. freedom and justice

Immigration Stations: Compare and Contrast (p. 49)
Alike: Both were located on islands. The purpose of both stations was to process immigrants before they entered the United States.
Different:
Ellis Island: Ellis Island operated from 1892 to 1954. Located in New Your Harbor on east coast of United States. Major port of entry for European immigrants coming to the United States. Today, Ellis Island is part of the National Park System.
Angel Island: Angel Island operated from 1910 to 1940. Located in San Francisco Harbor on west coast of United States. Major port of entry to the U.S. for Asians and other immigrants coming to the west coast from the Far East. Today, Angel Island is part of the California State Parks system.
Conclusion:
(Answers will vary.)

Migration & Immigration History Activities — Answer Keys

National Immigrant Heritage Month: Drawing a Conclusion (p. 51)
Map: Millions of immigrants have settled in the United States. As of 2018, most immigrants settle in metropolitan areas of the United States. The cities along the east and west coast of the United States have the largest immigration populations. New York City on the east coast and Los Angeles on the west coast have the largest immigration populations.
Pie chart: The United States has a large immigrant population. Over 13 percent of the people living in the country are foreign born. National Immigrants Day and National Immigrant Heritage Month help us remember the history and achievements of immigrant communities across the nation.

Unit Four: United States Citizenship
The Constitution and Citizenship: Locating Information (p. 53)
Multiple Choice
1. B
2. A
3. D

Fill in the Blanks
4. the process by which immigrants become citizens.
5. a person who is recognized as a legal member of a country.
6. 1868.

Fourteenth Amendment
7. The Fourteenth Amendment placed citizenship under control of the United States government, defined a citizen of the United States, and established rights of citizens and requirements for citizenship.

Naturalization: Word Meaning (p. 55)
Native Citizen: a person who was born in the United States; also a person born outside of the United States to a parent or parents who are U.S. citizens
Naturalized Citizen: a person who immigrates to the United States and then becomes a citizen
Green Card: entitles the person to permanently live and work in the United States
Visa: entitles foreign students and visitors to enter the United States
Naturalization: the process by which immigrants become citizens of the United States
Alien: noncitizen

Rights and Responsibilities of Citizenship: Key Details (p. 57)
Definition: a legal member of a country and to have the full rights and responsibility of a citizen
Rights: protection from unfair and unreasonable actions by the government; right to due process of law; entitled to the equal protection of all the laws in the United States; right to be treated the same regardless of race, religion, or political beliefs; rights spelled out in Bill of Rights and other Amendments to the U.S. Constitution; and right of citizens to vote (if they meet the requirements)
Responsibilities: obey laws, pay taxes, serve in court, and defend the nation